Bayou

Bayou

Chris Helvey

A Wings ePress, Inc.

General Ficton Novel

Wings ePress, Inc.

Edited by: Jeanne Smith
Copy Edited by: Bev Haynes
Executive Editor: Jeanne Smith
Cover Artist: Trisha FitzGerald-Jung

Wings ePress Books
www.wingsepress.com

ISBN 978-1-61309-883-7

Published In the United States Of America

Wings ePress, Inc.
3000 N. Rock Road
Newton, KS 67114

Dedication

To Linda Voth, for making this book, and so many others, possible.

One

THE CLOCK HUNG on the wall behind the counter. The big hand was at the forty-eight-minute mark and the little hand was almost to twelve. A long mirror hung below the clock. If you looked in the mirror, you could see the front section of the Woolworth's store and a slice of the street beyond. If you bent your neck, you could see the bank across the street. I was sitting on the third stool from the end, drinking coffee and glancing at the mirror between sips. At two minutes till noon, I was going to walk across the street and rob that bank.

Not by myself, though. Johnny Lewis and Randy Sims were going to be inside with me, and Donald Baker would be waiting around the corner in the Dodge. Gladys Miller was in the Dodge, too. But she was waiting for me.

There wasn't much traffic on the street. A couple of kids walking along, chewing gum and kicking at cans. Under the awning outside the drugstore, two men in overalls were sitting on a wooden bench. The skinniest colored man I'd ever seen was leaning against an empty building next to the bank. His face was long and narrow and put me in mind of a half-starved mule. Now and then a farm truck rolled by and once a big, long black Cadillac that had to belong to somebody important. I took a drink of my coffee and glanced back up at the clock. Eleven-fifty.

Johnny and I had been robbing banks since the fall of '32. That was the year after my dad had lost the homeplace up in Platte County, Missouri, to the Bank of Weston and we'd had to leave the land that had been in our family for three generations. The rest of my family had gone to live with cousins or uncles, but my brother George and I had caught a ride with Lonnie Pepper to Kansas City and hopped a Santa Fe freight headed west. All that fall we'd bummed around Arizona and California, making meal money picking cotton or grapes, or doing roofing. Whatever odd jobs we could find.

As the weeks went by, the jobs got harder to find. By then the Depression had really taken ahold and was boring into the West like an auger. George had heard about timber work up around Seattle, and we were running for an open boxcar when it happened. It had started raining, not hard, but enough to put a sheen on the rails, so maybe he slipped. I don't know. George always was a little clumsy. Anyway, he was running behind me and I figured he'd be right along, or catch the next car. Only when I'd swung up and looked back to see if he needed a hand, all I could see was his legs sticking out from under the cars and the train picking up speed.

The waitress was coming over, working her way down the counter, smiling and chatting with the customers, trying to earn a tip. Tips had to be slim. Even with Roosevelt in office, the hard times had continued and whatever little a man might have had set back he'd had to have hauled out and spent by now.

Anybody could stand hard times for a while. Hard times naturally happened to everybody, but when they kept on, they got to gnawing on a man. Gnawing on him until they wore him down to bones and nerves. And when a fella got that way, he got desperate. Desperate men and women do lots of things they wouldn't normally even think of doing. Like robbing banks.

"Want a warm-up, mister?"

I smiled at the waitress and nodded. She wasn't hardly more than a kid, skinny, but with the dew still on. She had a long nose and crooked teeth, but I don't reckon she could help that, and she had a nice smile. Smiles were another rare thing these days. Hard times, by their very nature, wiped the smiles off people's faces and made them mean. Surely was hard to smile when you were tired and hungry and broke. Seemed to me, the longer the Depression wore on, the meaner people became. Last week I'd picked up a newspaper somebody had tossed down and read about a man out in Iowa who had gone to live with his uncle and aunt after his folks died.

Six months later, he'd killed them both with a meat cleaver and stole their Model A Ford and two hundred dollars they had hid back. Then he took off for California. Police had finally caught him outside of Omaha. The paper had quoted several people who swore they couldn't believe what he'd done. They all said he seemed like such a nice boy.

"Thanks," I said.

"You're sure welcome. Hot, ain't it?"

"Like blazes," I said, and it was. Been ninety or better for a week, every day, a degree or two hotter than the day before.

I glanced over the girl's shoulder at the clock. Seven minutes until noon, five until I started walking.

"Ain't from around here, are you, mister?"

"Only passing through."

She put her elbows on the counter and leaned closer until I could see the freckles on her face. "Must be nice to go somewhere new," she said, wistful like. "I never get to go anywhere. Only to work and then back home. Maybe church on Sunday, if I get up in time."

"Be patient," I said. "Someday, you'll get to travel." I glanced at the clock. Couldn't afford to get tied up in a conversation. Taking a last sip, I dug a dime out of my pocket and placed it on the counter. A nickel of it was hers. Enough nickels and she could buy a bus ticket to New Orleans or Vicksburg or Memphis. Travel was enriching. Heard a man say that on a street corner in St. Louis. You can hear a lot if you keep your ears open and your mouth shut.

I slid off the stool and started walking toward the open door. Had some traveling to do myself. I was aiming to travel across the street and rob the Merchants Bank of Louisiana. I counted on the journey being very enriching.

"Good luck," the girl called out, and I called back, "Same to you." Never could see where it hurt to let a person dream.

Two

I STEPPED OUT THE DOOR and angled down the sidewalk, crossing the street in the wake of a farm truck hauling a big-eyed steer. Out in the street, the sunlight felt like it was hot enough to melt you. If I hadn't been packing a revolver in a shoulder harness under my seersucker jacket, I'd have taken the durn thing off.

As I crossed, I looked up and down the street. Even a burg like Bryant City had a policeman or two. But I couldn't see them and Randy was walking into the bank. He was a big man and walked slow ever since he caught a slug in the knee in Paducah, Kentucky. I stopped and wiped my face with a handkerchief to give him time to get in position. I looked for Johnny, but couldn't see him.

Johnny and I had been together ever since he saved me from a bad beating on the San Pedro docks. When I asked him why he'd done that, he'd grinned big like he does and said that I reminded him of an old friend. That was right about the time everybody started turning mean and it was safer if you had a partner to cover your back. Since it made sense, Johnny and I had partnered up.

At first, we'd worked legit. Potatoes in Idaho, teen wheat in Kansas. After the wheat, we'd helped the Southern Pacific build a bridge across the Rio Verde River. When that was done, we'd heard about work with sugar beets in Colorado, but once we got to the fields, we found out that harvesting sugar beets would flat out make a man's back ache. Two days after we started, we stole a pistol out of a pawnshop in Denver and took up bank robbing. At the time, it had seemed romantic.

I glanced up the street one final time and saw the mule-faced colored fella was staring at me. He had yellowish eyes and they were staring at me like I was a ten-cent freak in a sideshow.

I choked down the urge to pull out my Colt and shoot him right between his yellow eyes. That colored made me nervous. My guts were telling me he was bad news, and I chilled off some right then, even standing in the middle of the street with the sun beating down on my head. Wished I had time for a smoke, but I heard the courthouse clock striking the hour and started again. All the way to the bank, I could feel those yellow eyes staring at me.

Inside the bank, the air was still hot, but at least the sun wasn't beating down on you and a ceiling fan stirred the air. Once inside, I paused, blinking as my eyes adjusted. When they had, I could see Randy in line behind a woman in a blue dress that was too big for her. She looked like a girl wearing her mother's clothes.

It wasn't much of a bank. There were only three lines. Johnny wasn't in any of them, and I turned around in time to see him walk through the door. He didn't even glance at me. Johnny was dressed sharp in striped pants, two-toned shoes, and a white shirt. He was carrying a briefcase like he was a businessman. When we first hooked up, he looked like any other hobo. Over the years, he'd changed.

A young clerk was sitting at a desk on one side of the lobby working on a ledger book, and he glanced up as Johnny walked by. Johnny smiled at him so big you'd have thought they were cousins at least. The clerk nodded, but I noticed he didn't smile. Hard times made hard people.

Johnny got in line behind an old fellow leaning on a cane. Despite the heat, the old man was wearing a suit and something in the way he held himself made me think of a preacher. I bent down and retied my shoes, killing time till Johnny got to the front of the line. By the time I'd finished, the preacher had wrapped up his business and was walking toward the door. That was all right, but what wasn't all right was a guard coming out of a door I hadn't seen at the rear of the bank. He was buttoning up his fly and paying no attention, but all that was about to change.

I eyeballed Johnny, half intending to say something that would make him step out of line, but I saw his back stiffen and knew he'd seen the guard. The guard was sloppy looking and on the chubby side, but I could see the handle of a pistol poking out of the holster. Fat boys can still shoot.

Johnny stepped on up to the counter and set his briefcase on it, opening the case so that only he could see the inside. I slid a hand inside my jacket. At the edge of my vision, something moved, but at that moment, Johnny pulled his pistol out of the briefcase and showed it to the clerk. One line over, a woman choked back a scream.

"Now, everybody be quiet and nobody will get hurt." Johnny nodded at the guard. "Just take it out slow, buddy, and put in on the floor gentle like. Then push it toward me."

Johnny was speaking softly and the bank had gone so quiet that I could hear a car rattle by on the street.

I had my gun out now and knew Randy had done the same. He liked pointing a gun at people. Randy was a jittery boy and made me nervous. Sometimes he made me long for the days when it was me and Johnny, but they had been afore people turned so mean.

With three guns drawn, the guard didn't have a chance and I watched him pulling the revolver out of his holster slow and extra careful, and started to breathe easier. Only I wasn't easy in my mind. Maybe it was the heat, or that yellow-eyed darky who stared at me, or too much coffee, but my nerves were trying to send me a message.

One minute everything was going exactly the way we'd planned and the next it was like hell had come to Bryant City.

Guess it was that clerk. Dude never had seemed quite satisfied. Should have kept an eye on him. All I saw was a blur of movement off to my right before a gun blasted out and women started screaming and men started cursing. I whirled around.

The clerk was scurrying around the side of his desk, looking Randy's way and I figured he hadn't spotted me yet. You bet I kept my eyes fixed on that desk. It was like waiting for a squirrel to pop his head around a tree trunk.

But the kid never waited till he got around the desk. Instead, he popped up before I was ready and started blasting away. I shifted aim and pulled the trigger.

So many guns were going off it sounded like a small war. Guess Johnny and maybe the guard were shooting, and I knew Randy and the kid were firing away. Plus, I was squeezing the trigger. Maybe other men were shooting. Sure enough sounded like it.

I wasn't sure of anything, though. I was yelling and cussing and my eyes kept blinking. My legs were trembling and sweat poured out of me. If war was like this, I didn't want any part of it. The army could stick its medals where the sun don't shine.

Suddenly the kid screamed once, pirouetted like a fancy dancer, and sprawled out across his desk, his white shirt turning red. For the first time, I turned and looked around. Randy was sitting down, with his hands pressed against his stomach. Johnny was backing up with his gun in one hand and the briefcase in the other. I couldn't see the guard at all.

I ran across the room, shouting at everybody to get down. My voice sounded high and strange, like a rogue wind was carrying it away from me. When I got to Randy, I could see right off it was bad. Blood was flowing over his hand he had pressed against his gut.

"All right," I said, "let's get you out of here." I slipped one arm around his back and started to tug. Should have used two, but my gun was in the other one.

"Don't," he moaned. "I can't make it. You go on."

"Come on." I pulled on his arm. "You can do it."

"No way," he said and settled back against the wall. "I'm done for. Get the hell out of here."

"Damn it, Randy, come on."

I could hear Johnny shout something, but I was trying to pry Randy off the wall and onto his feet. Then I heard the siren wail, gave Randy the goodbye look, then started running.

Everybody in the bank seemed to be running toward the front door. Everybody except for Randy, and the kid sprawled across the desk, and the old man who looked like a preacher. He stood in the middle of the floor with a bewildered look on his face. I couldn't see Johnny.

The siren was closer now, wailing like a wild animal in pain. The afternoon seemed to be crashing down around me. I couldn't see Johnny, and Randy was dying, and I was starting to doubt getting out of Bryant City alive.

The old man who put me in mind of a preacher was standing there with his mouth wide open and his eyes skint back in his head. His lips were moving, but he wasn't making any noise. Grabbing him by an arm, I spun him around and shoved him in front of me. As I stepped out into the sunlight, I heard somebody moan. Randy or the kid, it didn't matter. The dead and dying weren't my problem, not anymore.

The first face I saw outside the bank was that of the skinny colored man who'd been leaning against the wall. Bastard had a damn .22 rifle in his hands and was swinging it up to sight me in. I snapped off a shot on the move, and chips and dust flew off the bricks above his head. What the hell did that yellow-eyed son-of-bitch want to be a hero for anyway? People were changing, getting so that I couldn't begin to understand them. Nobody knew their place anymore; that was a big part of the problem.

The old man stumbled and I got an arm around him and pulled him so tight against me that I could feel his bony shoulder blades poking against my chest. He wasn't tall enough to give cover to my head, but as a shield, he was better than nothing.

Women were screaming and the siren was piercing the air and kids and dogs and running men seemed to be everywhere. I was trying to keep the old man moving and find Johnny at the same time. The police cruiser was cutting down the middle of the street, big and black, rolling fast.

I started backing down the sidewalk. Thirty yards away was the river and all I could think of was to try to get across the river, although I couldn't see clearly what good that would do me. Still, you never knew; if a man simply kept going, sometimes he caught a break.

The cruiser whined to the curb and three cops spilled out, drawing their weapons, shouting for me to drop my gun. Giving up my gun wasn't something I aimed to do. Giving up that gun was a sure-fire one-way ticket to prison.

I'd never served time in anything bigger than the Memphis jail, but that was enough. I couldn't do any more time. Not at thirty. When I lined up all my tomorrows, they didn't stack high enough to cast much of a shadow.

I looked around for Johnny, half expecting to see him dead or handcuffed. All I saw was angry, scared faces. A dog trotted down the middle of the street with his tail curled in the air. The old man was praying and calling on God. Preacher Man had pissed his pants. I could smell the acrid odor and told myself that if I got half a chance, I'd push him off the bridge. Baptize the old son-of-a-bitch.

Cops kept yelling for me to drop my gun. Telling me everything would be okay if I'd only toss the gun away and then lie down on the sidewalk. Yeah, and like my daddy had told me a hundred times, people in hell want ice water. I kept backing down the sidewalk, glancing at the crowd every few seconds, but I couldn't see Johnny or Gladys or the car – only cops and a crazy colored with a .22.

If Johnny or Donald didn't come rolling up soon, I was screwed. I couldn't imagine where Johnny was, but Donald should have been rolling at the first crack of gunfire. Movement caught my eye, and I glanced up the street. Inside the frame of an open window on the third floor of a brick building, a man stood peering down the barrel of a rifle. Looking straight at me, ready to pull the trigger if the old man stumbled.

I was going to die. Could feel death in my bones. Die in a lousy Louisiana burg in the middle of a baking hot day.

Just as I was trying to decide whether to run or give up or shoot it out, the Dodge came around the corner, rolling in from a side street I hadn't noticed. Pulling the old man along, I began backing toward the curb. Sunlight was branding the back of my neck.

I kept moving, tugging the old man along, trying to keep one eye on the car and one on the crowd. I'd lost sight of the police and that worried me.

When we'd first started robbing banks, it hadn't seemed nearly as dangerous. People were so surprised to see men with guns in a bank that they'd offered us virtually no resistance. A couple of the tellers had even smiled as they handed over the money. That had only been the training kicking in. Training, and the small-town sweetness you could still find for a few months after the crash. In Chicago, say, or Kansas City or Dallas, any big city, it might have been different. But now the whole world had turned mean. Even in a hick town like Bryant City, the people had turned mean. Damn Depression had gone on until it had turned people hard and cold-hearted—the way fire tempered steel.

Sweat was trickling down my cheeks, and I could smell the old man's piss. One man in the crowd had on a bright yellow shirt. In all my life, I'd never seen such a yellow shirt. Funny what a man will notice when he's fixing to get shot.

One policeman ran down the sidewalk on the other side of the street, crouching low and ducking behind people. Close by, a woman screamed, and I turned my head in time to see the car pull to a stop near the curb. Pulling the old man after me, I stepped down onto the street.

"Hurry up," Johnny shouted and just hearing his voice I knew I was going to make it. Always could count on Johnny.

Nowadays, everybody needed somebody to cover his back. Johnny and I had been through so many hard times together it seemed as if nothing could ever pull us apart.

I kept easing backwards, the gun pointed at the old man's head. He was crying now. I could hear his sobs above the crowd. The crowd made a throbbing noise, like a giant motor coming to life. My leg bumped against the side of the car and I risked a quick glance behind me. Gladys was opening the back door. Donald was behind the wheel, his face tight and set, his eyes fixed straight ahead. Johnny was in the front seat and he had the Tommy gun out and pointed at the crowd. Taking a deep breath, I shoved the old man away and dove into the back seat. Somebody snapped off a shot and the bullet pinged off metal.

Over the back of the seat, I could see one of the policemen. He had one foot on the asphalt and he was crouched in a shooting position. I pointed my pistol at his chest and fired through the back window. Glass shattered. People screamed and somebody close cut loose with a shotgun.

Three

THE ROAD CURLED UPHILL, wound around the crest, as though the men who had built it had become confused, then turned sharply south and ran as straight as a well-plowed furrow for over a mile. Then there was the state line. You drove across the line and the road surface changed and you were in Mississippi.

That was the way Johnny and I had always robbed banks. Some folks even called us the State Line Bandits. Before Randy and Donald. Even before Gladys. We only robbed banks in small towns within a few miles of a state line. We'd robbed banks in Kansas and Missouri, and Arkansas and Illinois, and Kentucky and Indiana. Now we'd robbed a bank in Louisiana. Years ago, we had decided not to rob any banks in Tennessee so we would always have a state we could go to and lay low if the heat got too much. We'd been to Tennessee twice. Randy had an uncle who lived outside Nashville. During the week, his uncle worked in a feed store. On the weekends he preached at a holy roller church.

For some reason, Randy's uncle had never liked Johnny. Once he claimed he saw the devil in Johnny's eyes, but I figured that came from reading Revelations after midnight. Even though Randy's uncle didn't like Johnny, he put up with him for Randy's sake. He knew Randy had strayed from God, but as a preacher he also believed in forgiveness. At least he'd preached about it often enough. Some nights even at the supper table. Don't believe he thought much about me, one way or the other. My mind drifted back to Randy in the bank with his bloody guts in his hand. That deal with his uncle was shot to hell.

Up ahead was a big square sign that said *Welcome To Mississippi!* I turned and peered over my shoulder. All I could see was the highway and a thin line of old trees. On the other side of the trees was a barbed-wire fence. Beyond the fence was a meadow. Wildflowers grew in that meadow and black cattle grazed there. Grass in the meadow had grown so high it rubbed against the bellies of the cattle. Seeing the cattle put me in mind of Texas. When I'd been a boy, I'd longed more than anything in the world to go to Texas and be a cowboy. Later on, I'd wanted to be a baseball player.

The car was weaving, crossing over the center line before it drifted back. It was as though Donald was going to sleep. Letting go of Gladys's hand, I leaned forward. Johnny was gazing into the sack of money. Donald's head nodded. The car slowed and drifted for the side of the road. In Mississippi, the road shoulders were sandy and the tires slid as they hit sand.

Johnny's eyes shifted toward Donald and he stared sliding across the seat, grabbing for the wheel. Donald's head wobbled, then fell over. Put me in mind of a tree falling. It fell quite slowly, and when it hit the side of the door it bounced.

Johnny steered us down the shoulder. He couldn't get over Donald's body to reach the brake. You could hear the tires swish through the sands. For as far as I could see. Mississippi was as flat as a table. It was as though we were on a carnival ride. Gladys' fingernails dug into my arm. You could smell the warming asphalt and the honeysuckle that grew wild along the road and the hot coppery scent of blood. Gradually, the land began to rise and we coasted to a stop. There was the feeling of being on a ride to the end of something and now you were there.

Johnny shifted into park and I gave Gladys a quick hug and stepped out of the car. I peered in through the window at Donald. Blood stained his shirt. Looked as though he'd spilled a can of paint. Blood had pooled on the seat and his mouth was open. His eyes were like polished glass. A breeze had come up and it ruffled his hair in a way that put me in mind of corn silks fluttering. Once, in Indiana, I'd seen corn silks move like that and I wished I was back in that field.

"What happened?" Gladys' voice was squeaky.

I looked back at her. She was trying to keep from crying. "Caught a bullet," I said. "Bled to death. Must have clipped an artery. Lucky to make it to Mississippi."

"He had to know he was hurt bad. Why didn't he say something?"

Johnny leaned his head back against the seat and looked up at the sky. "Donald never was one to say much. Guess he knew his time was about up, and what good is talking then. It's not like we were family."

No, I thought, we weren't family, but we weren't strangers, either. If we'd known, we could have tried to help, or at least said a few kind words. Only I doubted we would have. Not with the cops shooting at us. In the end, though, it didn't matter. Words couldn't save a man from dying. Nothing could save you when your time was up.

"Guess we'd better get him out of here." I looked across the car. Horseweeds grew high and thick between the road and a line of trees. Blackberry bushes had grown up in the grasses. A pine had come down in a windstorm. Most of the needles were still on the branches. "Let's carry him over there behind that fallen pine."

Gladys made a face. "Aren't you going to bury him? Donald should have a proper burial."

I started walking around the car. "Sure," I said, "we'll bury him. No shovel and once the word on the bank hits the wires, every cop in Mississippi will be searching for us. Sure, we'll bury him."

I motioned to Johnny and we each grabbed a leg and pulled him across the seat. Johnny gripped Donald's legs and I got under his arms and we carried him through the high weeds. I kept glancing back at the road, but our luck was still running good.

A dead body always seems heavy, heavy and cold. Donald hadn't been dead for more than five minutes, but already his skin had a clammy feel. I was glad when we curled around behind the downed pine. A faint scent of pine still lingered. We eased Donald to the ground. His eyes were still open and I didn't close them. Lying in the grass and flowers, he looked young—younger than I'd ever seen him look.

"How old you reckon he was?"

Johnny shook his head. "Don't know. Don't recall I ever asked." He made a face. "Guess it don't matter much now anyway."

"No, don't guess it does. You want to say a few words?"

"Go ahead."

I tried to think of the right words. My mind felt hollow. Time ticked like a mantel clock inside my skull. It seemed to be beating way too fast. A blue jay started squawking somewhere in the trees. I knelt. Kneeling somehow seemed the right thing to do. At least I could do that. Weeds brushed against my face and sweat ran down my spine, dampening the crack of my ass. "Rest in peace," I said and stood up.

Flies had already found the blood. All the way back to the car I could hear them buzzing.

Four

THE AIR WAS the color of moldy grapes and a whippoorwill had started up across the road. I was sitting at the window, hoping for a breeze, remembering how full of death this day had been. The kid in the bank, the security guard, Randy, Donald. Too much death for my mind to handle. How men in war did it, I couldn't begin to comprehend. Some didn't. Teddy Beech, the oldest son of Old Tom Beech who ran a grocery in Weston, had come back from France a different man. After the war he always had a nervous look about him, glancing down a lot and flinching at loud noises. Made you think of a dog who'd been kicked one too many times.

Maybe you became used to death, I thought, the way you become used to the shape of your nose or the growling in your guts when you hadn't eaten in a couple of days, or the lonely sound of a train whistle late at night. Right then I wished I was on a train, and it didn't matter where it was headed, as long as it was rolling on down the line.

Gladys was sitting on the bed, counting the money out of the one bag Johnny had grabbed. She'd already counted it three times. Three hundred and seventy-six dollars. Came out the same every time she'd counted and it would come out the same again. Three hundred and seventy-six lousy dollars and Randy and Donald both dead. What a stinking, lousy trade.

Johnny was lying on the bed, shoes still on, smoking Chesterfields and staring at the smoke drifting toward the ceiling. Not over an hour ago we'd pulled into the tourist camp; since then he'd smoked four cigarettes. Couldn't blame him.

Gladys wiped sweat off her forehead with the back of a hand and shifted position on the bed. The springs squeaked.

"Damn, it's hot in here. Don't this place have an electric fan?"

"Take some clothes off," Johnny said.

"Ha-de-ha-ha. You're a fine one to talk, laying on the bed with your dirty shoes on and smoking a nasty cigarette. Aren't you truly about to burn up, Johnny Lewis?"

"Nope, I'm cool as cucumber in Grandpappy's patch."

"Oh, you're a funny man, you are. Can't you see how much I'm laughing?"

Johnny ground out his cigarette in a glass ashtray and rolled over on his side facing Gladys. Only he wasn't looking at Gladys, he was eyeballing me.

"Ah, Gladys," Johnny said, "you're purely working too hard counting all that old money. Ain't that right, Ray?"

"Sure," I said, "that's right. Any way you slice it, money's hard work. Making it, counting it, it's all hard work."

"Spending it ain't, smarty pants." Gladys grinned like she was a homecoming queen.

"That's where you're wrong, baby. 'Cause once you spend it you've got to go back out and make it some more."

"That's your job," she said and laughed. I liked her laugh. It sounded like sleigh bells.

I pushed up out of the chair. My shirt was stuck to my back. "Sun's going down," I said. "Want to take a walk?"

Gladys lifted her eyes and smiled. But she shook her head. Her blonde hair swung left, then right, looking like straw blowing in the wind. "It's simply too hot to be walking, honey. Besides the mosquitoes are out. I can hear them whining. No, I'm gonna stay here and count this money. Surely, I'm miscounting. Has to be more money than three hundred dollars."

"There is," Johnny said, "there's seventy-six more dollars."

"Oh, you," she said and swatted at him as though she was smacking a fly. Thinking of flies made me remember the flies buzzing Donald. Didn't say anything, though, only crossed the little room, pulled the door open, and stepped out into the twilight. Johnny and Gladys were laughing about something. Maybe laughter was good for them, but it didn't seem right to be laughing so soon after so much death. Today, it had been like losing two family members. One thing about the Depression, it had created a whole lot of strange new families, families that never would have even been dreamed of before.

The humidity was up and Gladys had been right about the mosquitoes. One landed on my cheek and I smashed at him. When I pulled my hand back there was blood on my palm.

The tourist camp stood along a narrow strip of asphalt that wound through a long patch of scrub pines and sassafras. Hardwoods stood there, too, but they were few and far between. Creepers had crawled up the trunks of most of the trees and wild grapevines grew as thick as a man's arm.

A stream ran beyond the cleared ground. In the dusk, I could hear it gurgling. Frogs croaked and deeper in the woods an owl hooted. A man named Lukenkamp ran the tourist camp, but the name on the sign on the shoulder of the road read *Jacob's Court.* Pulling a cigarette out of my pocket, I jabbed it between my lips and lit it with a Fire Chief match. My old man had always sworn by Fire Chief matches. Should have buried him with a box of 'em. I blew smoke out my nostrils and started walking toward the sound of moving water.

Underneath the trees the air was dead still. Mosquitoes whined and small creatures of the night rustled in the underbrush. I slapped at the mosquitoes and kept moving. Others had been there before me and barely enough daylight remained to show the path. The water smelled closer than it sounded, and when I stepped out from under the canopy of leaves I was on the slick riverbank.

The very last light of day frosted the top of the water. I didn't know the river's name, but it ran deep here, flowing with a subtle swiftness. On my side of the river, an old sycamore had fallen and its branches trailed in the water like fingers of a giant. I sat on the trunk and watched the moving water, trying to imagine where the river had begun and all the miles it had traveled and where it was going. Figured that somewhere down the line it would flow into the Mississippi and wind on down to New Orleans and the Gulf of Mexico.

Mexico sounded nice. Maybe I'd go there after this was all over. Surely the Depression couldn't go on forever, although it seemed to, even with Roosevelt telling us the only thing we had to fear was fear itself. Well, good for you, Franklin D., I thought, but all your talk was so much manure wrapped in cellophane with a curly ribbon on top.

Hunger was what a man had to fear, hunger and poverty and homelessness and loneliness. Loneliness most of all. If he had family or friends, even one, a man could stand an empty gut, and he could keep moving, even if it wasn't to a job, and he could sleep in a haystack or a barn or on the bank of a smooth flowing river. It was the loneliness that got to him, that ate his guts and his mind like a cancer, that killed him slowly and painfully. Bullets meant a quick death, loneliness a miserable one. Better to die like Randy and Donald than like my grandpa had, stomach cancer killing him so slowly that you could sit there and watch him wasting away until you thought he surely wouldn't last the night, only to come back a month later and there he was, still dying. Couldn't rightly call that living.

I thought about Gladys and Johnny back in that lousy motel room and Randy dead on a slab somewhere and Donald already starting to rot behind a dead pine tree in a state where nobody knew him or cared a bit more for him than they did a Jersey cow. Actually less, because a cow, no matter how stupid and stinking, at least gave milk.

Loneliness was coming down right then like a fine spring rain on that bank of that river I couldn't name. I could feel it splatter on my shoulders and drip down my face and I dug in the pockets of my pants and pulled out my old harmonica and pressed it against my lips.

I'd bought the harmonica in Joplin, Missouri, the day after our first bank job in Oklahoma. It had been early morning. Fall had been coming fast and the wind was out of the north. The sun was out that morning, though, and the glitter of the sunlight off the cornets and saxophones had caught my eye.

Music had always been a part of my life. Uncle Tommy had played the guitar and one of my cousins had sung in the church choir. I could even recall hearing my mother play the piano. But since she had died on my fourth birthday, maybe those memories were really nothing more than wishing dreams.

Not that I was any great musician, but I could play a little. Mostly blues tunes I'd picked up in the Kansas City clubs and a few Jimmy Rodgers songs. Once in a while I fooled around with creating a new tune.

I licked my lips and started blowing. Harmonicas make a lonesome sound if you hold your mouth just right and control your breathing. Lonesome and sad – exactly right for a quiet summer night alongside a river you'd never seen before, and probably would never see again.

It was all that skinny colored's fault, I thought. Somehow that yellow-eyed son-of-a-bitch had cursed the job. Colored people always gave me the creeps. People like him were a hell of a lot of what was wrong with this country. Never had liked different sort of people. Even before a half-breed shot my cousin in an alley off Neosho Street. Damn skinny bastard, probably put some African voodoo curse on us.

I could feel the hate and the anger inside me raging up like a fire that had been stoked, and I knew that was no good. What the hell good was it to get angry on a riverbank at night by yourself? I concentrated on the harmonica and tried to recall the day I'd met Gladys.

She'd been waitressing at a crossroads café in Indiana. Cornfields had stood green and thick on all sides and her eyes were the color of the Hoosier sky that August day.

Noticed her the first minute I'd walked in. Johnny was getting the oil changed in the Ford we drove in those days and I'd gone on into the café, planning on a cup of black coffee and a hamburger with onions. Only somewhere between the coffee and the hamburger, she'd given me a look that made my mouth go dry, and I'd asked her what such a pretty girl was doing pushing java and pie to farm boys and truck drivers.

Right then, without evening blinking an eye, she'd leaned over the counter and let me have a peek down her waitress uniform and said, as plain as if she was talking to the preacher after Sunday services, "Waiting on the first exciting man to come in off the highway and take me away."

"Well," I'd said, once I'd got my throat unstuck, "guess I'm one right exciting man."

And she'd laughed and said, "I hear that line every day of the week and twice on Sunday. Now tell me, mister, just what in the world makes you exciting enough to take me out of this little patch of paradise."

Then I'd leaned in close, looked her square in those blue eyes that made my heart ache and said, real quiet, so only she could hear, "My buddy and I just robbed a bank in Illinois. Exciting enough for you, Mabel?"

She'd done strange things with her eyes and then said, "The name's Gladys, and are you for real, or only making fun of me?"

"Gladys," I'd said, "I'm about as real as it gets," and lifted my shirttail and let her see the butt of my pistol.

For a minute she didn't say a word and I was afraid I'd gone too far too fast. Then, she got a truly serious expression on her face and leaned so close her hair brushed my forehead and said, "Eat your burger, and then you and your buddy pull around back and open the door. That is, if you outlaws want some female company."

After those words, she stopped talking and, for what seemed the longest time, we simply stared at each other across that counter. Felt like we were staring straight into each other's soul, seeing everything, good or bad, we'd ever done. Weighing each other in the balance, you might say.

Neither of us said a word. Finally, I'd picked up my coffee and nodded at her through the steam. Not more than twenty minutes later, Johnny had wheeled us around back of the little cinderblock café and I'd pushed the door open. She'd come out the back door still wearing her waitress uniform, walking like a princess. When the screen door slammed behind her, I'd wondered what the cook was thinking, but there wasn't time for worrying because Johnny was already spinning gravel and raising dust. Thinking back on what happened that day, it didn't seem quite real. But Gladys was real enough for any man.

As if I'd conjured her up from dusty memories, I heard her calling my name. Pulling the harmonica away from my lips, I called out, "Over here."

I waited for her to come, but she must have changed her mind. I heard the screen door to the cabin slam shut, and then a truck highballed it down the highway, headed south. She was a changeable woman.

Five

GUESS I MUST HAVE DOZED, 'cause I came awake to the sound of a train whistle, long and lonesome, and part of me wished I was on that train, whether it was passenger or freight. I'd done my share of riding the rails. I shook out another cigarette, lit it up, and took a long drag, holding the smoke for a moment before blowing it out. We hadn't eaten hardly anything all day and my stomach was growling. Some days a man has to get by on smoke and dreams.

The door to the cabin swung open and Johnny stepped outside. I knew it was him by his whistling. Nearly every night when it got dark he started whistling. Always whistled the same tune. He'd told me the name once, but all I could remember was that it was a slow dance tune from the '20s. It was like that song had gotten stuck in his mind and the only way he could get rid of it was to whistle it. Lots of nights I wondered why he remembered that one special. Figured a woman was involved.

Johnny whistled it all the way through, started again, but cut it off short. In the silence I could hear the tree frogs starting up and birds settling for the night. The moon was up and stars were starting to come out. I figured Johnny was hunting for me, so I whistled like a quail.

I watched him walk down the path. Even in the filtered moonlight I could recognize his walk. When you've been around a man every day for three years, you learn his ways. He looked up like he was seeing a message in the stars and then he stepped into the deep dark under the oaks.

"What you doing out here, Ray?"

"Smoking, smoking and remembering," I said.

"Remembering what?"

"Remembering when we picked up Gladys."

"Yeah, I recall. Hey, give me a smoke."

I shook one out and passed it to him. He pulled a box of matches out of his shirt pocket and lit up. The smell of phosphorous clung in the still, heavy air and then it was joined by the aroma of burning tobacco. For a couple of minutes, we smoked quietly, not saying a word, each man thinking his own thoughts, staring at the stars or back across his life, according to his tastes, just like we'd done hundreds of times.

Finally, I asked the question that had been nagging me all day. "How come you reckon things went so bad this morning, Johnny? Think that colored man put a spell on us?"

Instead of answering, he took a drag off his cigarette. I wondered what he was thinking. He had his silences and they went deep. Never had figured out what was going on in his mind. There'd been a lot of silences lately, but I couldn't figure what that signified. The train blew its whistle again and then the owl started up once more, deeper in the oaks. We both cocked our heads and listened to the hooting swirling up out of the dark. Sweat trickled down my forehead and onto my nose and I reached up and wiped it off.

"Old owl sure makes a spooky sound, don't he?" Johnny said.

A mosquito whined at my ear, then settled on my cheek. I smashed him. "Some old timers claim an owl is a bad sign."

"Sign of death is what I heard."

"That's what they say, but surely we've seen enough dying for one day," I said. Then we both fell quiet, listening for that owl. But the only night sounds were the swish of the tires of a late-travelling car out on the highway and the croaking of a bullfrog covered by darkness.

"So, you don't want to talk about it?"

"Talk about what?"

"This morning."

"I don't know what went wrong. Didn't see no coloreds. Plus, I don't believe in that voodoo nonsense. Anyway, there's not a damn thing we can do about it now. Yeah, I know Randy and Donald are dead, and I hate it like hell. But, in the end, so what? We made it out all right, didn't we?"

"Yeah, we made it," I said, "but we shot that kid and the guard. We never shot nobody before."

"That couldn't be helped. The kid was stupid, plain stupid. As for the guard, he had to know the risks he was taking whenever he strapped on a gun. Life's full of risks. We all take 'em."

I took a final puff and ground my cigarette out on the trunk of the sycamore. "Sure, the kid was stupid, but I've got a bad feeling. Like our luck is running out."

"Oh hell, Ray, you're always thinking and feeling too much. Get yourself all worked up in knots and nine times out of ten there's nothing to it."

"Maybe so, but I vote we lay low for a spell. Take a few months off."

"Now why in the hell would we do that? We decided months ago that we'd keep going until each of us had enough money saved back to do what we wanted. As I recall, you was looking to buy some land back in Platte County and I was thinking about opening me up a little bar in Kansas City. Remember? We talked about how I'd come out to the farm to see you and you'd bring your wife into town and have a drink with me at my place. Johnny's Three Aces, I'm going to call it, after a hand that won me the biggest pot I ever saw. That was in Tulsa at the old Rheinlander Hotel, up on the tenth floor, back in twenty-seven. One of those games that started on Friday night and lasted till Monday daylight, or until everybody but one was tapped out. Dutch Stromeyer used to run those games."

Johnny took a hit off his cigarette and tapped his foot against the trunk of the closest oak. "Wonder if old Dutch is still alive?"

"Why wouldn't he be? He wasn't that old."

"True, but times have changed. Depression's made every business tougher. Lots more competition now. No factory jobs and the farmers can't pay the hands wage enough to live on. New blood, see? Hungry men all across the country, just roaming around, searching. Men who are just as likely to take what they want with a gun as not."

"Like us."

"Yeah," Johnny said, "like us."

I wiped off more sweat, wishing I had a hamburger, even a cheese sandwich. Johnny didn't seem to be sweating. He never sweated much.

"I'm not saying quit forever. Only lay low till the heat blows over."

"What heat? I don't hear no sirens. Aw, come on, Ray, you know we've got the system. Rob a bank as close to the state line as we can, get out of town in a fast car, and be across the state line before the cruddy bankers know what hit 'em."

"I'll admit it's been working, but we never killed a man before. Killing puts a whole new light on it. Police spotlight, if I don't miss my guess."

"So what? Those rubes will never catch us. Did you see that old Ford they were driving? Motor was smoking before they got out of town."

"Yeah, but there's telephones and telegraphs, and now the damn FBI is catching just about everything except the wind."

Johnny punched my arm and laughed. "Well, they've never caught us, partner, and they ain't never going to. Long as you and me stick tight we've got it made. We're a team, sure enough. A team with a system. Now, come on, only a few more banks and it's back to Missouri for the two of us."

"What about Gladys?"

"Sure, we'll take her along. Good looking woman changes our image. People, especially the police, won't be expecting that. Besides, it's almost like you two are married, always hugging and kissing on each other like a couple of fool kids." He punched me again. "Now, partner, you know I'm right. Just like always," he said and started laughing.

Johnny had a good laugh. One that made you feel like it was a pure pleasure simply to be alive. Still, I had this queasy feeling that something wasn't right. I turned my head and spat into the dark. In a way he was right, but I simply didn't like the plan anymore. Didn't feel comfortable like I did before.

Maybe I was getting old, or maybe it was seeing Randy shot to pieces, but for sure something wasn't quite right. Been feeling something was off for weeks. Nothing I could place a finger on, but still it was there, like a gravel in your shoe.

I didn't argue. Wouldn't have been much use in it. When it came to arguing, I couldn't hold a candle to Johnny. But I knew what I was feeling deep in my gut. Gut thinking hadn't let me down yet. But sometimes it took a while to figure out exactly what it was trying to tell me.

Maybe if Gladys hadn't stepped out of the cabin right then I'd have kept pushing on Johnny, made him open up, and things might have turned out way different. But the cabin door swung open and a bar of light fell onto the yard and Gladys stepped into that light. I peered through a break in the trees and there was her blonde hair, glimmering in the dark.

Johnny and I both turned and looked at her and she sure was pretty with the light falling on her hair and making it shine. She'd gone blonde in Kentucky and I liked that. Since the first moment I saw her in that café up in Indiana, I'd thought she was about the prettiest thing I'd ever seen. Turning blonde only seemed to make her even more special. Blonde hair makes me think of icing on a cake.

She started walking toward the car, calling our names and Johnny gave a shrill whistle. She whirled around and came running through the moonlight. She ran right up to me and threw her arms around my neck and kissed me on the mouth. Her lips were warm and her breath smelled like the peppermints she was forever sucking on.

"Oh, baby, guess how much?"

I kissed her back. "I don't know, how much?"

"Well, it's three hundred and seventy-six dollars. Divided three ways, that's, let's see, a hundred apiece, and seventy-six dollars for gas and eats and incidentals. Isn't that wonderful?" She kissed me again.

"Now what you going to do with one hundred dollars, Miss Gladys?" Johnny asked. Gladys had made me forget he was there, and his voice startled me.

"Oh, Johnny, I don't know. Simply don't know what to do," Gladys squealed. Then she reached over and gave Johnny a hug. He winked at me over the top of her blonde head, and grinned like he knew something the rest of us didn't.

I didn't say anything. Only wished he'd go back to the cabin so I could be alone with Gladys. Ever since we left Louisiana I'd been wanting her, and the waiting was getting on my nerves.

"Come on," Gladys said, "let's go back inside and I'll give everybody their share."

"Sounds good," Johnny said.

For some reason, and to this day I'm not sure why, I didn't want to go back in with them right then. Maybe it was because I was still remembering that kid bleeding to death on that desk so each of us could have a lousy hundred dollars, with seventy-six for gas and eats and incidentals, as Gladys said. Or maybe I was simply in one of my moods, aggravated at Johnny. Lately, he'd had an attitude that rubbed me like roughed up concrete. Anyway, I said, "You two go on. Want to smoke one more and then I'll be along."

"Suit yourself," Johnny said. "I'm going to get in there and get my money in my hot little hands. I'll hold those dollar bills all night and have the sweetest dreams."

Gladys snuggled up close and kissed me. After she finished, she whispered, “Hurry, honey.” I kissed her back extra good and squeezed her arm.

Then they turned and I watched them walk side by side out into the moonlight. Walking that way in the night they made a handsome couple. Halfway there, Johnny draped an arm over her shoulders and a second later I heard her laugh.

When the cabin door had closed, I leaned back against the tree and listened to the bullfrogs croaking and the mosquitoes whining. A few minutes later, I heard the train whistle one last time. The train was far off now, heading west, and its whistle sounded to me as though the earth itself was moaning.

Six

SMOKE BURNED YOUR EYES WHILE MUSIC blasted your ears. Strands of lights drifted down from the ceiling and stretched across the room like orange and red spider webs. The band, if you could call it that, was a couple of coloreds singing blues tunes, with a few old standards thrown in, only jazzed up. The drummer was the blackest man I'd ever seen, while a high yellow played saxophone. Every few minutes, a mulatto midget wandered up on stage and jangled a tambourine or a string of bells for a song or two. Then he would jump off the stage and stumble back to his chair in the corner. He appeared drunker than hell.

The band had switched to a slow song and Gladys and I were dancing. Well, we were swaying around the dance floor, trying to keep from bumping into the other dancers. A dancer I wasn't, but slow dancing was all right. Gladys was a good dancer and her body felt soft against mine.

"Hot in here, isn't it?" I whispered in her ear.

"Oh my, yes. I'm soaked. I'll have to wash off again before we go to bed."

"Want to go outside a while? Take a walk?"

"No, I want to keep on dancing."

"In this hole?"

"What's wrong with this place, Ray?"

"You ought to ask what's right about it, Gladys. It's nothing more than a cruddy road house in west Mississippi, full of smoke, too loud music, and a bunch of coloreds and drunks running around."

"You old sourpuss, there's plenty of white folk in here, too. Coloreds is only playing in the band and cleaning off tables and such. And I think the music's pretty good."

Wrapping my arm a little more tightly around her, I pulled her close and kissed her cheek. She tasted of face powder and sweat. "Come on," I said, "let's get out of here and I don't mean a walk. Let's go find us someplace to spend the night besides that durn car, and in the morning we can drive on down to New Orleans. I'll take you to one of those swanky places in the French Quarter. Music and the food will both be better, not to mention there will be a whole lot better class of people around."

"Ah, honey, what's your rush? I like it here. I'm having a good time and I want to dance here till they close. Haven't danced in weeks. Not since Louisville. All we've been doing is driving and robbing banks and killing people. That shit gets old in a hurry."

"Keep your voice down, Gladys," I whispered in her ear. "This place is jammed. No telling who's here. Might be a sheriff right here on the dance floor."

"Oh, Ray, you're no fun anymore. Why don't you just hush up and dance?"

"All right," I said and pulled her so tight against me that I could feel her breasts mashing against my chest. Maybe I was hurting her a little. I wasn't sure, but I squeezed a little harder.

"You're about drunk," I said as we whirled around and around until the room was spinning. I was glad when the song ended. Tell the truth, I'd had one too many myself. We swayed together as we walked off the dance floor, then stepped apart.

Johnny was holding our table down, grinning like he'd just heard a good joke. "What a lovely couple. Energetic, too. Maybe we should enter you two in one of those dance marathons."

"And what's wrong with dancing, Mr. Johnny Lewis?"

"Why nothing, Miss Gladys."

"Good. Then get up and dance with me. Old Ray is a pure sourball tonight. No fun at all."

The band struck up another song, one with an up tempo, and I sat down. Johnny got up and led Gladys back out onto the floor. Dancing and drinking at a west Mississippi road house wasn't my idea of laying low. Not only did you not know who was at the next table, you were spending money on whiskey and beer, not to mention fried chicken and biscuits. Spending it like water. Blood money, too. At least the way I saw it.

I leaned my chair against the wall and watched the people gyrating around the dance floor. They looked like refuges from a tribe of Australian Bushmen. Up on the makeshift stage the colored drummer had gone crazy. Man was beating the holy hell out of his drums. Beads of sweat stood out on his face like raindrops and when he shook his head, water sprayed across the stage. He was so black he appeared purple.

My glass was empty, but there was a pool of liquid at the bottom of Gladys' glass. I picked it up and drained it. Then I eased my chair down and pushed up. My shirt was sticking to my back and the room was swaying gently. Putting a hand on the table to steady myself, I glanced across the dance floor. The band had gone back to a slow tune, "Tallahassee Serenade." It was an old tune. One you used to hear back in the good times. Maybe that's all anybody was trying to do, I thought, rediscover the good times.

Johnny and Gladys were slow dancing on the far side of the room. She had her head on his shoulder. All the couples were slow dancing. It was a slow, sad song and it made me want to cry, cry for all those lost good times.

The midget had climbed back on stage and this time he was playing a harmonica he'd drug out of the back pocket of his overalls. Dude must have been wearing kids' overalls. Or maybe his old mammy had made him some special. He didn't look like much, but the man could play. I had to give him that. For a minute I stood still, listening, fixing the tune in my mind so that I could replay it whenever I wanted that sound. When I had the tune down, I turned and walked across the roadhouse, swaying a little. Sweat dripped off my face.

Seven

NIGHT AIR WAS STILL, HOT, AND MOIST, sweet with the scent of honeysuckle. The parking lot was graveled I crunched across it, swatting at some of the moths heading for the gatherings around the security lights set atop creosoted poles. Maneuvering between parked cars, I tried not to step on the broken bottles.

Cars and pickups were arranged in raggedy rows. Men and women sat in some of them. In spite of the heat, or maybe because of it, in some of the vehicles the couples were so close together they appeared as one creature. In others, they sat on opposite ends of the seat, each leaning against their own doors. Some were smoking, while others drank, or talked, or kissed. In a battered Model A, a man sat slumped behind the wheel, snoring gently.

Away from the roadhouse the air grew cooler and I could hear the gurgle of moving water. At the end of the parking lot, I stepped off the gravel onto uneven ground. Out here the light was almost gone and I took the first steps slowly, stumbling once when the ground gave way.

Gradually, my eyes began to adjust and I could make out a narrow path. Bare earth shimmered in the moonlight and I followed it. The path curled as though it had been laid out by a snake, or a drunk, but it kept moving down the slope and before long I could see moonlight reflecting off water.

In the quirky light, the stream looked small enough to jump. Willows grew along the bank, their branches drooping until they touched the water. Sycamores grew there, too, bigger around than four or five men and rising fifty feet in the air.

Voices murmured further on down the bank and I found a stump and sat down. Inside my skull, my brain was still spinning and my tongue felt thick and heavy. I didn't want to see anyone, so I stayed where I was, staring at the water, trying to sober up.

In a minute, footsteps sounded behind me and I glanced back up the slope. A man was coming down the path, whistling softly. He had a bottle in one hand. He walked like he'd come this way before. I sat quietly.

At the bottom of the path, he paused and took a swig. Then he turned and headed toward me. I was sitting in deep shadows and at first he didn't see me. Then the light, or his angle of sight, changed, and he stopped short.

"Well, hello there," he said.

"Hi."

"Hot out tonight, ain't it?"

"Sure enough," I said, shifting on the stump until I could see his face better.

"Not from around here, are ya?"

"Nope."

"Know how I could tell?"

"How?"

"Your accent. You might be a good old boy, mister, but you sure ain't from Mississippi. Nor Louisiana neither." He took a step closer, easing out into a patch of moonlight, until I could see his long, bony face clear.

"Accents is a hobby of mine. Getting them right, that is. Started when I was in the war. Got sent to France on one of those troop ships near the end and they had us all mixed together without any rhyme or reason. 'Course, that was the Army for you. Biggest percentage of what they did made no sense at all." He took another step and cocked his head to one side. In the moonlight, his face looked like a squirrel's head that had got caught in a vise.

"Was you in the Army, mister?"

"No, never got called up. Had a cousin who volunteered, though. Got shipped out the week before the Armistice. Shipped all the way to France, then turned around and came home without even landing."

The man laughed, his braying harsh in the night. "Well now, ain't that the way of this old world? Some serves, and some tries to serve, and some don't get called at all." He snorted. "Kind of like religion, ain't it? Some folks hear the call of the Lord and answer. Others hear, but ignore it. Then there's those who ain't never heard the call."

He bent his neck and peered down at me. He was close enough that I could smell the sweat on his body and the liquor on his breath. "You heard the call of the Lord, mister?"

"No," I said, starting to wonder if this man was drunk, or crazy.

"Thought I did once," he said, shaking his head, "but guess I was mistaken. Or else I got lost. You ever get lost?"

"Everybody gets lost, one time or another."

The man laughed again and took a swig out of the bottle. Then he offered me the bottle. I didn't really want another drink, but didn't want to offend the man either. With strangers you truly never knew. Taking the bottle, I wiped off the lip with a shirt sleeve and took a slug. It wasn't rot gut, but it wasn't the good stuff, either.

"You ain't lost, are you?" he said.

I handed the bottle back to him. "Don't think so."

"I mean you're travelling through, ain't you? 'Cause I know you ain't from this part of the country. Being sheriff of this county, I know damn near everybody, and I don't recognize you. You ain't got the accent. Midwest, I'd say. Maybe Kansas."

"Close," I said. "I'm from Oklahoma." I'd started to tell him Missouri, which would have been the truth, but something held me back. These days it paid a man to not blab everything he knew. "I'm going down to New Orleans. Got an uncle there. Said he might could find me work on the docks."

The man's teeth were white against the night. "Well now, that's sure fine, ain't it? So many men begging for work and you've got a job already lined up. And in New Orleans, too. Your uncle an important man?"

"No, but he knows the man who hires men by the day for dock work."

"Well, you be careful traveling, you hear? Ain't safe nowhere these days. Crazy people driving around, shooting people, robbing banks. Can you believe it?"

"According to the news, men are robbing banks all over the county. Times are so hard lots of men figure they don't have any other choice, I suppose."

"Hard times don't give any man a right to kill another man. Why, over in Louisiana, barely a mile, maybe two, across the state line, a bunch busted into a bank couple of days ago and shot it to hell and back. Killed a clerk and a bank guard. Clerk was only twenty-one. Don't you think that's a damn shame, killing a kid for a few dollars? See, the damn hoodlums only got away with a couple of hundred dollars."

Right then I almost spilled the whole pot. Too much liquor, perhaps, but I nearly said, "Naw, it was almost four hundred." Now, that would have been like showing up at the penitentiary and begging them to let me in. Instead, I coughed and spit out, "Crying shame."

The sheriff nodded, his jaw hacking at the dark. "Still, the criminals didn't get away free and clear. No sir, not at all. One got gut shot right in the bank. Took him a day and half to die. Must have been one tough son-of-a-bitch. Police claim they shot the car up pretty good. Said they didn't see how the driver could have made it."

"Did he talk any? The one that got shot, I mean."

The sheriff shifted on the stump and stared at me. The sense that he was seeing through my skin and bones, straight into my heart, made me feel as if all my clothes had fallen away, leaving only skin and bones.

"Why you interested?"

I shrugged. "Merely curious. Doesn't make any difference to me," I lied.

For a moment I thought he wasn't going to answer. I could hear the stream gurgling behind him and, more faintly, music, faster now, the rhythms pulsating across the night.

Then he nodded, turned his head, and spat as though he had a bad taste to get out of his mouth. "Turns out he didn't say much, unless you count 'Go to Hell'."

I smiled in the dark. "Well," I said, "guess I'd better be going. New Orleans, you know."

"Son, you know something?"

"What's that, Sheriff?"

"I think that would be an extra fine idea."

I could feel my guts tightening up. Wasn't sure how much of what I told him he believed. But I was sure the sooner we started moving the better. "Thanks for the liquor," I said as I turned and started back the way I'd come. All the way up the slope I kept waiting for the other shoe to fall.

Eight

Thunder rumbled low off to the west and I rolled over and sat up. It crackled again and I slid off the bed and eased over to the window. I didn't know the time, but the night had that post-midnight feel. Lightning forked across the sky, illuminating the darkness. The storm was still across the river, but already you could smell the rain.

We were holed up in some tourist cabins in Mississippi, about as far west as you could go and still stay in the Magnolia state. Johnny was trying to line us up another job. We were just across the state line from Braxton, Louisiana, laying low for a couple of days to let what was left of the heat from the law dissipate and have us a little vacation. Johnny and Gladys were drinking about every night now. Hitting the stuff pretty hard and going into town for dances. Dancing wasn't my idea of a good time and going to town seemed dangerously chancy to me.

Johnny only laughed and told me not to be such an old fogey. He claimed this next job was a sure fire big one. Maybe *the* big one and we'd have to be dodging every hick sheriff, cop, and state trooper south of the Mason-Dixon Line for weeks. Said we'd better have us a few good times now. I just didn't think the same way.

Between claps of thunder, I heard Gladys roll over in bed and I turned and gazed at her sleeping form. Her face looked like a small pale moon. One breast had escaped from her gown and her hair hung across her face. Longing grew in me like a river rising. We hadn't made love in almost a week. One night Gladys had been too tired. The next night she'd had a headache. The third night—well what difference did it make?

A shutter banged against the side of the cabin and the white curtains blew in at the window. After the heat of the day, cool air was a blessing. For weeks now the heat had been terrific. Each day a degree or two hotter than the one before. Couldn't remember a hotter summer.

The day before, the car had broken down with a shot fan belt and Johnny and Gladys had elected me to walk to town and buy a new one. The walk had taken two hours and all the time I'd been sweating like a race horse and so damn thirsty that when I came to a pool of water at the edge of a culvert, I'd scraped the algae aside and cupped up the water. It had been warm and tasted of minerals, but it had beat dying of thirst.

My eyes were starting to adjust and I could see her lips were parted and the tip of her tongue stuck out in one corner. Her bare arms flowed like milk and the curve of her hip made something inside me tighten up.

Crossing the room, I eased back on the bed. Gladys didn't move and I kissed her lips so softly I might have been the night wind. She stirred in her sleep, but didn't open her eyes. My fingertips caressed her bare breast. Thunder hammered against the dark wall of sky and shafts of lightning lit up the room. Rain began to fall—hard and fast, as though it had been gunshot from the clouds.

"What you doing?" she murmured. Her voice was thick with remembered sleep and her eyes were still closed.

"Being friendly."

"Well, don't."

"Why not, honey?"

She reached out a hand and pulled my fingers off her breast. "I just don't feel like it tonight, that's all."

I rolled over on my back and stared up at the ceiling. All I could see was a vague dull whiteness, as if a cloud had floated into the room. "You never seem to feel like it lately."

Gladys stayed quiet on her side of the bed. I rolled back over and kissed her on the cheek. Might as well have kissed a fireplug. I edged back to my side of the bed. For what seemed like a long time, we both simply lay there listening to the thunder. Sounded like it was moving off to the south, but rain was still hammering the roof. Gladys had grown still and quiet. I couldn't hear her breathing. I raised up on one elbow.

"Go back to sleep, Ray," she said, sounding the way my mother used to get when us kids didn't mind her. I didn't want to start thinking about the old days again. Those memories made my head ache. There was no going back, not to those days, not to the old times, not to the good, sweet golden times before Hoover and his damn Depression. Hoovervilles, I'd seen enough of to last three lifetimes.

"Go to sleep, Gladys," I whispered. Then I eased out of the bed again and walked over to my clothes and dug out my cigarettes and a box of matches. I struck a match and the business end blazed up in the darkness, flickering like one of the candles the Catholics were always lighting. I lit the cigarette, took a drag, and blew smoke out in a long stream, feeling the heat of it going across my tongue and lips. Then I wandered over to the window. Leaning against the wall, I watched the lightning playing down toward the Gulf.

Confused as hell, that what I was. Nothing seemed quite the same as it had been. A nagging slice of me wondered if I was starting to lose my mind. For sure, I wished things were the way they used to be. Back when Randy and Donald had been alive and we'd never killed anybody. Back before all the drinking and dancing. Back when we were nothing more than a few souls trying to rob our way out of Hoover's Depression. Thunder rolled, faint now, sounding like rail cars coupling in a train yard miles away. I was naked as the day I cried my way into this old world and it was raining all over west Mississippi.

Nine

I COUGHED, spat, and kept walking down the sidewalk. It was late afternoon and the sun was starting to slip behind the tallest of the buildings. Shadows had fallen on the pavement and broken their backs, then regained strength and slithered across the road. Johnny and I were casing a bank in some village in Mississippi. Though it was July and the heat was fierce, I felt cold inside, as though ice was floating through my veins.

The bank stood on the corner across the street. It wasn't a big bank and I wasn't clear on why Johnny felt we needed to do this job. My brain felt thick and I couldn't remember the name of the town, but it started with a G. There was one paved road and couple of gravel ones. A courthouse stood in the center of the square. The courthouse looked like it hadn't been painted since the Civil War.

For a week he'd been yammering at me about doing another job and I'd been yammering back about laying low for a few weeks. What sounded like the best plan to me was following up on the tale I'd told that sheriff outside that roadhouse. Drive on down to New Orleans and try to find work on the docks. Of course, I didn't have an uncle, but I wasn't afraid of manual labor and New Orleans was a busy enough port, even in the hard times. If nothing else, it would put distance between us and that nosy sheriff. Best I'd been able to do was talk Johnny into doing was driving a hundred miles south and never staying too long in any one place.

Johnny glanced at the courthouse, then shifted his line of sight to the bank. "Farm town, so say we hit it on Saturday."

"Johnny, maybe we ought to give this one a pass."

He turned his head and started at me. "Have you lost your mind? Why would we not bust this cracker box?"

"It's too soon after the last job. John law is getting on to us. I told you about that sheriff."

"Damn, Ray, you're turning into an old woman. Scared of a hick lawman and a backwater town like this."

"I'm not scared of anybody, but there's simply no sense in taking stupid chances. That last bank in Louisiana was a warning for us."

"That was no warning, purely bad luck."

"I tell you it was an omen."

"Next you'll be telling me you believe in voodoo and witches."

I started to say something about pushing your luck, but a woman came out of a shoe store at that moment, so I nodded at her instead and started walking. To tell the truth, I didn't feel real good. In spite of all that Mississippi summertime heat, I was cold inside my body, chilled to the core. Cold sweat covered my face and my brain throbbed. The street seemed to tilt at a strange angle and I felt dizzy.

Except for once when I was drunk, I'd never passed out before, but right there on the sidewalk I felt faint. Tried to tell myself it was the heat, but I knew better.

At the end of the block there was a bench next to the sidewalk, under a live oak tree. The bench was in the shade. "Johnny, I don't feel so good. Reckon we could sit down on that bench for a few minutes?"

"What's the matter, Ray?"

"Don't know. But do feel like I'm coming down with something."

"Now, this ain't no trick to get out of the bank job?"

I stumbled and the world shifted. Then I blinked and everything came back into focus.

"No," I mumbled, "no." Seconds later, the world went to spinning and things went black.

Not sure how I got to the bench. Expect Johnny helped me. Vaguely remember sitting down and then every bone in my body starting to ache and my head growing hotter and hotter. Think I mumbled something, but can't remember what it was. Last thing I recall was easing my head down on the bench and some kids riding by on rusty bicycles, their fingers pointing at me.

Ten

I WASN'T SURE IF I was awake or asleep. My body felt like it was on fire. There was the sense of something valuable burning inside me. Even my brain felt like molten lava.

Sometimes I could see shapes, indistinct and wavering. Other times I couldn't see anything. Voices came to me, but I couldn't comprehend what they were saying. They were no more than voices from a fevered dream.

Time was passing. I could tell by the ticking inside my head. When I was a kid, we moved to town for a year or two, and an old lady lived down the street. Her name was Miss Edna Mae Mapes and she'd never married and always lived in the house she'd grown up in. Her mother and father had been dead a long time and Miss Mapes rented out their room by the week and another spare bedroom that had been her brother's and taught piano. In the fall, my brother and I would rake up the leaves that had fallen from her ginkgo tree and burn them. When we'd finished, she would give us a dime apiece and a dish of cobbler. Usually rhubarb. I still like rhubarb cobbler. On her piano she kept a metronome. She would let us eat our cobbler in her living room, thumb through her picture books, and listen to her metronome. For years I'd wanted to learn to play the piano. Miss Mapes' metronome was ticking inside my head now. Hearing that ticking made me wonder if I was as dead as Miss Mapes' mom and dad.

Fever dreams came as visions that floated in from nowhere I could place and made no sense: dreams of men riding dogs and moons floating on moving water, dreams of boats that ran on dry ground and stumps that spoke in foreign tongues. Yet, in my dreams I could understand every word the dream people uttered.

Now and then I dreamed Johnny or Gladys was bending over me, mopping my forehead with a soft cloth, or giving me a drink of water. Maybe those moments were reality. I didn't know; I could only guess. Perhaps they were fever visions, and maybe it was better if they were.

Without warning, I awoke with my head as clear and cool as hollow ice. Sweat covered my body and my shirt was soaked. My mouth was dry and my tongue felt thick in the dryness. I knew I wanted a drink of water and tried to get out of the bed. But I was so weak I couldn't move.

Instead, I lay there, letting my body and mind drift further from those crazy dreams. It was evening. I could tell by the light. I was lying on a narrow bed jammed against a plaster wall. Across the room, a window was set into the wall, and when I lay on my right side I could see out. From the bed, all I could see was a tree limb covered with branches, with a slice of blue sky above. A bird swung back and forth on the limb. Merely a small bird, dull brown and short-tailed, but he was singing. If I raised up on one elbow, which was all I could do, I could see a meadow full of tall grasses and white flowers and beyond, a line of scraggly timber.

I wanted to get up and get a drink, then go stand at that window and gaze out at the world. However, it felt as though all my strength had drained away while I'd dreamed. A strange, peaceful acceptance flowed through my veins as I listened to the bird singing, trying to figure out where I was, watching the light fade. When it was almost dusk, the voices came. At first, I thought was simply dreaming again, but then I remembered I was awake and started listening hard.

At first the voices were far away, hardly more than evening murmurings and I'd half convinced myself I was dreaming after all when I recognized the voices. Have no idea what made me do it, but I shut my eyes. Maybe the fever had left me afflicted, or perhaps I was starting to slip out of consciousness. Anyway, I shut my eyes. Seconds later, the little bird quit singing. Then I heard a door screech open, followed by footsteps. They fell soft, as though whoever made them was tiptoeing.

No one was talking now, but I could hear those soft footsteps on the wooden floor, and now and then an old board screeched where a nail was working loose. Keeping my eyes closed, I tried to breathe smooth and steady, like I was asleep. Can't say for certain why I acted that way. Maybe I sensed something instinctively, the way a wild animal does. Or maybe I only wanted to hear what they had to say without them knowing I was listening. Or it could have been that I only wanted to surprise them and see their faces when I opened my eyes. The fever was back on me and my mind was starting to swirl.

If they'd moved more slowly, I think I'd have spoken. One minute longer and surely I'd at least have opened my eyes. In fact, I was thinking about doing exactly that when I caught a whiff of her perfume.

Gladys didn't wear perfume often, but when she did, she always smelled of lilacs too long in bloom. I'd smelled that scent often enough to recognize it from the grave.

"Still asleep, exactly like I figured."

"Sure enough," a man said softly. A second later, I knew it was Johnny who had spoken. That's the way my mind was working then. In low gear. Fever brain, my grandparents would have called it.

"What if he don't make it, Johnny?"

"Oh, Ray will make it all right. Bastard's too tough to die from the pneumonia."

"How do we know he's got pneumonia? He might have influenza, or some weird fever."

"Doesn't matter. It ain't gonna kill him."

"But what..."

"I don't know. Something will work out. Always does."

"How long you going to wait?"

"I'll know when the time's right," Johnny said.

The room went quiet then and I lay there listening, waiting for them to start talking again. But all I could hear was that metronome ticking inside my head and, from far off, cattle mooing. I cracked one eye open. From where I was on the bed it was hard to see anything. At first, all I could see were shadows moving across a wall. Then the shadows turned and I could see them.

Gladys had her back to me. Her face was pressed against Johnny's chest. His arms were around her shoulders and he was rubbing her back under her dress, while he stared across the room and out the window. His eyes had that faraway look, as though he were seeing something the rest of us could only imagine. I thought I saw his eyes shifting toward me, and I closed mine tight. But then, maybe that was only my imagination working. Fever can do strange things to a man's thoughts.

When I opened my eyes again, the light had gone out of the room and only the afterglow remained. A whippoorwill had started up outside and a cool breeze floated in through the open window. I was alone in the room, although a hint of the lilacs remained. I lay there listening to the whippoorwill, trying to decipher what had been a dream and what had been reality, and what I should do next. In the end, I told myself it had all been my imagination and rolled over on my right side and stared out the window as the world grew dark and the metronome ticked inside my brain. After what seemed like hours, the whippoorwill fell silent and an owl started up down in the line of second-growth timber that rimmed the meadow. Hearing the owl reminded me of when I was a kid. Then I knew I could sleep. Morning would be soon enough to decide.

Eleven

HOW LONG I LAY on that narrow bed in that little room I can't testify to. I slept; I dreamed; I awoke awash in sweat. Johnny and Gladys brought me water and soup, and sometimes they sat and talked and sometimes they came and then went away as though they were only a different variety of wind. Their voices I remembered, but nothing more. It was as though I was in a never-ending twilight.

But one morning when I awoke, my head was clear and the ticking of the metronome had ceased. I sat up and after a few seconds my head stopped whirling. It was that pre-dawn quiet when every sound is magnified and the world seems like it is being born again. In a strange, yet profound way, I, too, felt as like I had been born again. All my life I'd heard old folks blabber about being as weak as a newborn kitten. Now I knew how they felt.

Somewhere in the pale light, a bird twittered sleepily and a few seconds later another answered. My stomach growled and for the first time since the fever had struck, I was hungry. I swung my legs over the side of the bed and waited for the room to stop spinning. When it leveled out, I eased off the bed.

After being in the bed for so long, it felt strange to be standing. My legs were trembling and I took a wobbly step and got one hand against a wall. Planking was smooth against my palm. Standing there, I realized I was barefoot and shirtless. All I was wearing was my pants. I let my eyes drift around the room, but couldn't see my shoes or shirt. I took another step, sliding my hand along the wall. Then one more. After the fifth step, I quit leaning on the wall. I was moving now, not swiftly, but plodding the way a tired fighter does when he's heading to his corner after a tough round.

Beyond the small room where I'd been staying was a larger room, perfectly square and completely empty. The next room was the kitchen. A wood-burning stove stood in one corner and there was a table pushed against one wall with a couple of chairs wedged under it. A bowl of apples stood on the table. The apples were dull red and going soft. Fruit flies swarmed them. A ledge, about as wide as a piano bench, ran along one wall. On the ledge was a tin pail, with a dipper hanging over the edge. I crossed the room and peeked inside the bucket.

The water looked clean, and I dipped some up and smelled. It didn't smell like anything. Suddenly I was very thirsty. Shutting my eyes, I let a trickle of water run over my lips and tongue. The water tasted like nothing more or less than water, only cooler than the room, as though it had been recently pulled from a deep well. I took a longer drink. Then I filled the dipper again and drank every drop.

My thirst eased, I began to hunt for something to eat. The apples were too far gone to be appealing, but at the end of the counter was half a loaf of bread and a hunk of cheese.

The end of the bread was dry, but I found a knife in a drawer and cut off the end, then sliced two thick pieces. Next, I cut three narrow slices of cheese and carried them outside.

Daylight was coming fast. Already the light was changing. The line of trees was still dark, but sunlight was starting to dust the meadow. Somebody had drug a chair outside and left it under a maple tree. I carried my bread and cheese across the grass and sat down on the chair. My legs were still weak.

It was pleasant to sit under the tree eating bread and cheese, listening to the birds waking, watching sunlight spreading across the meadow. Soon, I could see cattle in one corner of the meadow.

The house, actually nothing more than a shack, stood at the end of a long, winding gravel drive. Weeds and grass had grown up in the gravel, so I knew there hadn't been much traffic lately. At the other end of the drive was a fence with a wooden gate. The gate had swung open and the fence sagged. Beyond the fence was a gravel road. In front of the fence the roadbed was flat, but as it ran west it began to slope steadily upgrade. As I watched, dust began to rise from the far side of the crest of the slope. Seconds later, a car crested the hill and rolled down the slope. It turned in at the gate and came bouncing up the drive.

As both doors swung open, I jammed the last piece of cheese in my mouth. A cardinal flew toward the maple, winging hard from the tree line. Johnny and Gladys came walking across the patchy grass. They weren't walking together, but they were together. He was carrying a grocery sack. Her hair had grown out, and it was windblown and hanging down across her face. As she walked, she kept flipping it back with one hand. He was whistling a tune I didn't recognize.

"Well, well, well, if it ain't Lazarus raised up from the grave."

"Hello, Johnny."

Gladys bent down and kissed me on the check and suddenly it seemed like old times. "Feeling better, Ray?"

"Might live," I said reaching out to hold her hand, but she was already moving around behind me.

"Here, Gladys, take these groceries and go see if you can rustle us up something."

"Like what, Johnny?"

"I don't know, soup maybe, or some stew. Just go cook, okay. I want to talk to Ray."

"Sure, Johnny, sure."

I could hear her footsteps moving away. Then I heard the screen door creak open. Seconds later it slammed shut.

"She's a good girl," Johnny said, almost whispering. "Just a touch slow."

I didn't say anything, only stared out across the meadow. I'd been wondering how I'd act when I saw Johnny again. If I could only be positive what I'd seen and heard I'd know what to say. Or, if it all had only been dreamings I'd have known what to do. But certainty escaped me. Uncertainty robs a man of his will, and I simply sat there like a patient in a doctor's waiting room.

The cattle were plodding toward the house. Must have been twenty head. Looked to me like a cow's life wasn't all that tough. At least if you could put up with every kind of weather, liked to eat grass, and didn't mind ending up on display in a butcher's shop window. Then I thought about Randy. Guess it was thinking about butchers and blood that had called forth his memory.

"Good to see you up and around, kid."

"Good to be up."

"Couple of times there we thought we were going to lose you."

"Wondered myself once or twice."

"Reckon you had the Spanish influenza? That's what killed so many during the war, you know."

"That, or maybe pneumonia."

"Well, that might be. Not being a doctor, I couldn't say. All I know is I never seen a man sweat so much, and you was always crying out. Nightmares, we figured."

"Fever dreams, my grandma called 'em. Worse than nightmares. Seem so real you almost believe what happened in them was gospel."

"Remember any of 'em in particular?"

Truth was, I sorta did. But I wasn't one hundred percent sure, so I merely said, "Got a cigarette?"

He put one in my hand, and I stuck it between my lips and turned my head. Johnny flicked a match across a thumbnail and eased the flame against the end of the cigarette.

I drew smoke into my lungs and pushed it back out. After being so sick, it felt fine to simply sit in the sunshine and smoke a cigarette. Never would have figured on that.

"What have you two been up to?"

"Outside of doctoring and nursing, we've mostly been scouting around for another job."

"Find one?"

Johnny walked around and sat down on the grass and fired up a smoke. "Took a few days, but I've found us an extra good one. Little town called Porter's Junction. About twenty miles south of here. Not too big, say a couple of thousand folks, but big enough for a nice bank."

He looked up and grinned. "And get this, kid, they've got the lousiest security you ever did see. One old man so feeble he can hardly walk, and that's it."

I took another hit off the cigarette. "Don't have to walk fast to shoot a gun."

"Trust me, Ray. I'm telling you it'll take five minutes for this old fart to even clear his holster. But that ain't the best part of the deal. Not the real sweet part, I mean. Want to know what that is?"

"Sure," I said. Excitement was running through Johnny's voice like electrical current and I could feel my interest growing.

Johnny nodded like he was a teacher and I was a pupil who had given a correct answer. "Good, 'cause this one is sweet. And I mean sweet, brother. Sweet enough to make your mouth water. See, this Porter's Junction, it's not such a big place. But down the road, maybe six, seven miles from the bank, there's this gigantic fertilizer plant. Better than two hundred men work there regular and this plant, name's Bragg Fertilizer and Feed, pays every other Friday and let me tell you, it's one big payroll."

He paused and puffed on his cigarette. "Now, here's the kicker. Lately, there's been a mighty heavy demand for fertilizer. Now, don't ask me why. Never was a farmer and don't aim to become one. Anyway, there's been such a demand for this fertilizer they produce they've had to hire on extra help. Every blessed one of whom, of course, has to be paid."

"Should be a big payroll then."

"Biggest I ever saw. Add that to what's already in that cracker box of a bank and you're staring at a haul of twenty thousand, easy, maybe twenty-five. Think of all that split two ways, I mean three. Brother, this is the big one we've been waiting for."

"We could retire for life with that kind of haul, Johnny."

"Sure we could. And we will. Only you're going to have to help me. That monster payroll will be at the bank in two days. The big shots from Bragg's will pick it up the next day, so we can't wait. Think you can be ready in two days?"

"Sure," I said, although I wasn't. I still felt weak, and cheese and cigarette smoke weren't going to put me on my feet. Still, a man could improve a lot in two days. Without warning, a remembrance of the time I'd seen Johnny and Gladys in my sick room flickered across my mind. That vision came and went like heat lightning and a second later I was telling myself it had only been a fever dream. Deep down, though, I simply wasn't sure. Guess the way I saw it right then was that the hands had been dealt and we all had to play our cards. 'Cause there simply weren't any other cards to play. Least not that I could see. So, I said "Sure" again, took a drag off my cig, and stood up.

Reckon 'cause I stood up so fast, I started weaving. Johnny jumped up and grabbed my right arm, steadying me. Then he grinned and winked. "Let's go get some soup, partner," and we started walking toward the shack. Only I was still slow on my feet and we moved slightly out of step.

The cardinal had started singing and the scent of freshly mown hay was drifting on the wind. Sunlight was as warm as a winter quilt on my back. If we hadn't been making plans to rob a bank in two days, we might have been a couple of hands coming in from the field for lunch. Two brothers, say. As we stepped into the kitchen, I tried to think of two famous brothers, but my mind was still fuzzy and the only two I could name were Cain and Abel.

Twelve

I WAS SITTING on a bench in the sun, sweat sliding down my face like salty rain. It was so hot you could not safely put the palm of your hand on the hood of a car parked in the sun. Johnny was across the street, pretending to check out the seersucker suits in a show window. Gladys had just driven by and turned left. She would be coming up the alley that ran beside the bank any second. Plan was to have her idle there. At least she'd be in the shade.

It was going on for four o'clock, and in the afternoon heat, the traffic had died off. Except for a man who'd just hobbled by me, leaning heavily on his cane and looking like the last Civil War veteran, and a mongrel dog asleep in the shadows across the street, the sidewalks were empty. The old man had stared at me big-eyed, like he'd lost his mind. Fool had a head shaped like a walnut. It would have given me great satisfaction to smack his wrinkled Confederate face. Instead, I sat on the bench, sweating, and thinking about how sweet it would be to hear that walnut skull cracking open. Then I got to wondering what had made me so damn mean all of a sudden.

Down at the depot, a train whistle blew. As if that sound had been our signal, Johnny lifted his right hand. I nodded, and he turned and started walking toward the bank. I stood up, wiped the sweat off my face with the back of my hand, and started angling for the front door of the bank. Halfway across the street, I saw Gladys pull up into the alley. She eased the Ford forward until the nose almost touched the street. We'd ditched the Dodge weeks ago. The Ford wasn't the car the Dodge had been. But then it didn't have eleven bullet holes all down the driver's side either.

Gladys' face was turned toward me. But she was shading her eyes with her hands and I couldn't read her face. Johnny had told me they'd been practicing driving while I'd been sick, and that she could drive as good as Donald. That sounded fine, until you remembered that Donald had been blasted to his grave when he was behind the wheel.

I'd kissed her when she let us out of the car a couple of minutes after three o'clock. At the last second, she'd turned her head, and I'd got more face than mouth. She told me not to do anything crazy, and I'd figured she was simply afraid of catching whatever had laid me low. For the hell of it, I'd bent down and pretended to tie my shoe. Halfway through tightening the laces, I'd cut a sideways glance in time to see her and Johnny exchanging looks. Maybe it was all innocent. But it left me with the sense that I was missing something, and maybe had been for a while.

Then Johnny had asked her a silly riddle. Something about what did the baby porcupine say to the cactus? And she'd shook her head, all that peroxided hair looking like soft butter, and he'd said, "Is that you, Mama?"

She laughed and even I'd grinned and everything seemed fine the way it had always been and I told myself I was paranoid. Still, that missed kiss kept gouging. I shoved it as far back as I could. I had a job to do. Exactly like another other Joe. Only my job was that I had a bank to rob. Not that I particularly liked the job. Still, I was working, which during hard times meant something. Least I didn't have to beg from no man for a damn thing.

Since we were down to two men and a driver, I was going to have to cover for Johnny after he'd gotten the money. Wasn't crazy about being the last man coming out of the bank, but I couldn't see where we had any choice.

Porter's Junction sidewalks were wooden and raised about six inches off the ground. I stepped up and tromped down the sidewalk, boards screeching under my feet, the sound loud in the still afternoon. The only other sound was the echo of my footsteps.

I took a quick look both ways. All I could see was the sleeping dog and the old man. He was hobbling away from the bank. Tugging the revolver out of my pocket, I pushed open the heavy bank door.

The door squeaked as it swung open and the colored guy who was sweeping the floor looked up. I cursed under my breath. This one was a young buck, the color of coffee with cream stirred in, and he stared at me with his eyes squinched almost shut, his broom held at half-staff. Then he caught sight of the revolver and his eyes went wide and he opened his mouth like he was going to woman-scream. I shook my head and he shut it fast. Only he kept staring at me, and that made me nervous.

Nothing against them, but for me, colored people are bad luck. Not that any of them has ever personally messed with me, on purpose anyway. But I never have any good luck when even one of them is around. Over the years it's gotten so I can't hardly stand to even be in the same room with one. If the government left it up to me, they'd all be sent back to Africa or Asia or Mexico. Be among their own, see? Besides, America was supposed to be the white man's country.

Broom Man and I were still staring each other down, when I heard Johnny call out, "All right folks, this is a stickup. Just keep calm and hand over that Bragg's payroll money and the rest of the cash and everything will be copacetic. Now you," he nodded at the bank guard, who looked as old as Methuselah, "take that gun out of your holster and set it down on the floor, real gently. That's right, nice and slow. Now, take the side of your foot and nudge it over to me."

As the guard eased his gun out of the holster, a fat woman in a blue flowered dress caught sight of the pistol Johnny held in his hand and gave a gasp. Then she moaned and her eyes rolled back in her head. She went down like she'd caught a deer slug in the heart. Johnny eyeballed her lying on the floor like a side of beef and grinned. "That's right, lady, this is a gun and it's loaded."

Then he lifted his eyes and let them sweep across the handful of people in that little bank. "Now, the rest of you, sit down on the floor and cross your ankles. Keep 'em crossed and your mouth shut and nobody will get shot."

He pulled two burlap bags out of his briefcase and tossed them onto the counter in front of a woman with a thin, hungry face. For no good reason, I noticed she had a bad overbite. "Now, be a good girl and fill both these up for me. And honey, be quick about it."

You could see the woman's neck work as she tried to swallow. She finally got the knot down, picked up the bags and headed toward the vault. Her legs were trembling and the sacks shook in her hand. The vault door was cracked open.

I tried to keep one eye on the bank guard and one on the janitor. The bank guard was shaking like a demon possessed his limbs while Broom Man kept edging away. Him, I didn't trust. Never has been one a colored born yet that you could trust.

That damn metronome had started ticking again inside my head and my stomach was churning. Sweat covered my arms and face, but it was a chilling sweat. Nervous sweat, my dad would have called it, and maybe I was nervous. From the first, I hadn't liked this play. It was too soon after the last one and way too close to where we'd hit before. Best I could tell, we'd done a lot of zigging and zagging when we'd been driving, so that we weren't a hundred miles from the holdup that had gone all wrong.

The teller with the overbite was taking her time about filing the bags. Inside my head I was counting seconds. Like jockeys do in a horserace. I'd tested myself a few times against a stopwatch and never was off more than a second or two per minute. I was up to one hundred and forty-six. I could feel my finger tensing on the trigger.

"Hurry up back there," Johnny shouted. When there wasn't any answer, Johnny pushed through the swinging door and walked around behind the counter. Even though he probably could have seen inside the vault from where he'd been standing, I liked it better when he was behind the counter. You never knew when some glory hound was going to try something stupid. Something that might get us all killed.

All the customers were sitting on the floor like good little boys and girls. One woman had her rosary beads out and was fingering them. A little girl was holding her mother's hand and sobbing softly. I hate it when there are kids. Kids are forever finding ways to draw your attention. Everybody else was staring at the floor.

I was up to one hundred and seventy-three now and I took a step deeper into the bank and called out. "Everything okay back there?"

"Yeah," Johnny called back. "Just a whole lot of money here. She's filling the second bag now. Cover me, kid, I'll have both hands full of money."

I caught a glimpse of the broom moving and I whipped the barrel of the revolver around. "Move once more, spook, and you're dead. Now, drop the broom. Understand?"

He never hesitated, only let the broom fall, and I twisted back around to keep an eye on the rest. In spite of the afternoon heat, they seemed frozen with fear.

I'd lost count and started up again and got to twenty-six when Johnny came out of the back, walking with a burlap sack slung over each shoulder. Both must have been full of money. He was bent under their weight. Stepping deeper into the room, I made extra sure everybody saw the barrel of my revolver. In spite of the weight, Johnny was making tracks and he came alongside of me in seconds. I let him go by and counted to five before I started stepping backwards.

For a moment, I thought everything was going to be all right. Nobody had moved or made a sound and I could almost feel my share of that payroll in my hands. Maybe I was jinxing the job, thinking like that. But I couldn't see how. I was only thinking.

Perhaps I wasn't thinking straight. Or maybe I simply wouldn't let myself see. But things seemed so good right then that I let my guard down and backed on out that door. Nobody in that bank was moving one bit more than a bronze statue of Stonewall Jackson.

When I could feel the sunlight on the back of my neck, I glanced up the street and all I could see was that old mangy dog and, far off, that old Confederate on a cane. Both had turned around and were staring at me. But that didn't bother me one whit. The old man was too far away to identify me and that old dog was going to bite nothing. Everything was still going good.

"Keep coming," Johnny hollered, and I did. One step, two, and then I was stepping down onto the street.

"Hurry up, cop car coming."

I heard it then, the thin high whine of the siren, and I whirled around and flung myself in the back seat. Before I could get up to sitting, Gladys had us rolling.

I pushed myself upright about the time we whizzed by the old man. His mouth was wide open and his eyes were big. I didn't waste time on him, turning instead to check on the cop car. I could see it now, small and black in the distance.

"Step on it, Gladys," Johnny said. "That cop car has surely got more motor than this heap." I turned around to find him staring at me. His eyes were like blue marbles. "Get ready. We may have to shoot our way out of this town yet."

"Okay," I said, turning around and pointing the barrel of the pistol at the cop car. My right hand was shaking some and I braced it with my left. I could sense all that money in the gunny sacks beside me. Knew it was nothing but my imagination, but it seemed like the cash was putting off heat and a scent. It was almost like I could hear it breathing. Johnny had sure pegged this job. Never had I seen so much money in one place.

The cops were closing on us, but not as fast as I had feared. For a mile, the highway ran straight. Then it began to curl west. The cops kept closing some in the curves, so I fired off a couple of shots when the road was smooth. They backed off until they were nothing more than a black blur in the distance. Guess they didn't aim to get shot, even for the Bragg payroll.

We went through a sharp curve and came out at a crossroads and Gladys wheeled west again, and then west once more a mile or two down the road. We were out in the country now and the road had gone to dirt. Even for a country road, it was rutted up bad and the old Ford was taking a pounding. Cotton grew on one side of the road and big fields of sugar cane on the other, Now and then, I saw a milk cow or a swaybacked horse, and once I caught a glimpse of a white house on a rise of ground back off the road that reminded me of my home place.

I had no idea where we were and when Gladys wheeled down one narrow dirt road after another I was lost for sure. Johnny said something and she hit the brakes and pulled the Ford off onto a wide spot alongside the road. She sighed deep and cut the motor. I listened to it ping, not having a clue where I was.

Being lost didn't bother me. For a long time, ever since Dad had lost the farm, one way or another I'd been drifting. Lots of nights I'd gone to sleep not knowing where I was and in the morning I'd wake up not even knowing for certain what state I was in. So being lost didn't actually register anymore. Since I had no home, anywhere was home. But I didn't like this county. A raw open ditch, lined with poisonous looking weeds, ran beside the road. Beyond the ditch were a few scraggly locust trees. Several appeared diseased or dying. Behind the trees the land fell away sharply and you could hear water running.

I leaned forward. "What's the matter?"

"Car's starting to overheat." Johnny said. "Sounds like there's a creek over the bank. Reckon you ought to go get us some water?"

"Yeah, go on." Gladys said.

And why is it me that has to go, I wondered. But I didn't say anything. No use starting an argument. Besides, the bucket was on the floorboard by my feet. The old Ford had a bad habit of overheating, so it didn't surprise me that we'd had to stop for water. I picked up the bucket. Johnny eased forward and I pushed the seat up and stepped out, grinning. Only the day before I'd been wishing we could afford a new radiator. Now, we could simply ditch the Ford and buy us a new car. Any make and model we wanted. Cash money was the best money. I headed for the creek.

~ * ~

Beyond the trees, the ground slanted sharply downhill. Easy to see that the creek was one of those that flashes outside its banks after a hard rain. Flood waters had cut under the rocky ledge and carved out a cave-like depression. Horseweeds and brambles grew along the slope and only a narrow path led toward the water. I started easing down the path, placing my feet carefully and leaning back to keep from going too fast.

If you gave me ten thousand dollars in unmarked bills, I couldn't say exactly what made me look back. Maybe it was the rain crow who cawed so loud when I wasn't expecting it, or perhaps it was pure instinct, the way an animal, say a fox or a deer, senses things. Or maybe it was something in Gladys' voice, maybe nothing more than she hadn't said baby or honey or Ray when she told me to go get the water. I'd wondered when I heard her and guess that might have been worrying around in the back of my mind. But I couldn't swear to it. Not even for ten thousand dollars.

Still, I did turn around and peer back up the slope. I was halfway to the water and looking almost straight up, so that all I could see were two figures haloed by the sunlight. They put me in mind of paintings I'd seen of gods or Aztec chiefs. But they were only Johnny and Gladys standing at the edge of the bank. Johnny had something in his hand.

Sunlight filled my eyes and for a second I wasn't sure what I was seeing. Then I was and it felt like I'd swallowed a rock. Told myself I was being silly, but when Johnny raised his right arm, I knew I'd been right. Something was off, off bad.

Wasn't any use running. He'd simply shoot me in the back. If I jumped, he'd plug me before I could get my footing. I stared at him, wondering where it had all gone wrong. Money, or Gladys, or who the hell knew. Reason didn't matter. It was purely a crying shame it had come to this. But I'd be damned if I begged. I kept staring at him, trying to catch my breath. It figured he'd squeeze the trigger and get it over with. But he just kept pointing the gun at me while I kept staring into the round black eye of the barrel.

"Sorry, Ray," he said in a soft voice like there were people around and he didn't want anybody to hear. "Never intended it to turn out like this."

I was terrified. No use trying to deny that. Scared to hell and back. My legs were trembling as if the earth itself was shaking. My left eye was twitching and my mouth felt full of sawdust. If he didn't hurry, I was going to piss all over myself.

"Go ahead," I said. "Go ahead and do what you need to do. Only make damn sure you do it right." Why I said that, I don't know. Wasn't what I meant to say and it sounded stupid. At least my voice wasn't shaky. I was proud of that.

The muscles in Johnny's neck were corded up tight and his gun hand trembled.

Gladys nudged him. "Go ahead, Johnny, go ahead. Do it. We've talked about it for weeks now and I'm sick and tired of pretending. Sick and tired of kissing a man I don't even like. Do it, Johnny. Just do it."

Johnny drew himself up straighter and I wondered if I was bound for heaven, or for hell. I eased one step down the slope. It wasn't much. But sometimes one step is all a man can take.

"Do it, damn it, do it." Gladys waved her arms. I could see her body quivering, quivering like the aspens Johnny and I'd seen once in Colorado. That day flashed across my mind. It had been late in the afternoon, with the sky so blue it hurt your eyes and a cool wind had blown up with such force that it seemed like something alive. Right there in the middle of that sweltering Louisiana heat I felt a chill come over me. I wanted to live so bad I could taste it.

Trying not to be obvious, I started bending my knees. Now that the shock of seeing Johnny point a gun at me was wearing off, I figured it was better to take a chance on jumping. At least he'd have to shoot at a moving target.

I could feel my leg muscles gathering and twitching and a nerve jackhammered in my temple. I risked a quick glance sideways. As I peered toward the top of the slope, I saw a blur of movement and then the gun glittering in Gladys' hand. Without another thought, I jumped. Dove off the ledge might be more like it. Simply flung myself off, praying as I went.

Only I must not have prayed hard enough or said the right words, or maybe God was tired of the way I'd been behaving and decided to teach me a lesson. One second, I was as close to flying as I'm ever likely to get. The next, it felt like a hot hard wind blew through me, then curled back around and carried me away. Pain rippled through my left shoulder, but there was still the feeling that I was flying,

For a moment, there was only a weightless sense of being. Then my body smacked the ground and I rolled. I could hear myself screaming, but I kept on rolling. Then there was the sound of another gunshot, and a third.

My legs cracked into a tree and I scrambled to my feet, feeling the pain, moving like I was in a dream. Not sure how I did it, but I started running. Well, staggering might be saying it truer.

I heard Johnny shout and I remember bumping off trees and tripping over roots sticking up through the ground. Between the trees there were bare spots where the ground was dark and slick. Not quite mud, but close. My feet kept slipping and I wondered why Johnny hadn't shot me.

Then a bullet pinged off a tree beside my head and I jerked my head and stumbled for an opening between two willows. My hip grazed one of the willows and I lost my balance. I could hear water running and a rotting smell filled the air. The water had to be close. Another shot rang out and I expected to die. But I never heard the bullet—only Gladys screaming words I couldn't understand.

I remember that much. Then the world spun like a kid's top and I could see a hundred pinpricks of light and my shoulder was on fire. Felt like somebody had poured a gallon of kerosene over me and lit a match. Maybe I saw my mama's face. But I couldn't be sure because suddenly I was falling into a hole so deep and black that there didn't seem to be any bottom.

Thirteen

I COULD HEAR VOICES. Soft voices, murmuring like clear water flowing over smooth rocks. That was all – only those soft voices. For a long time, all I heard was those voices. I could not see anything, nor feel anything, nor think anything. The idea that I was dead began to take shape. And if I was dead then I was listening to the voices of angels.

Out of the darkness, light grew and with it pain. And I knew I wasn't dead, because no man who was dead could hurt so much. Pain smothered the voices and all I could think about and feel was the pain. Light was pressing against my eyelids. I could feel its heat, but I could not force my eyes open. There was only pain. My left shoulder, above my heart and off to the left, felt like it was on fire. Memories were drifting back now. I could sense them out there, crawling around in the darkness the way a coyote will creep around in the tall grass inches beyond the light thrown by a campfire's flames. Then the voices rose again, a man's and a woman's, and as I listened to them, recognition tickled. I cracked open one eye. It was the best I could do.

All I could see was grass and a few weeds and then the ground sloping up gradually. My legs felt wet and I turned my head an inch and I could see that I was sprawled out on a creek bank with my feet still in the water. Figured I'd floated downstream a few yards before the creek or river or whatever it was had washed me up. Not sure how I'd kept from drowning. Maybe I'd been conscious longer than I remembered.

At the top of the rise stood an old rail fence, with a huge gum tree growing so close that the branches were draping over the rails like wild hair. Behind it, the sun was setting and the light backlit the tree and fence, so that it looked like a scene out of a movie.

I could hear the voices all right. But the words were fuzzy, as though I was hearing them through cotton. Despite the pain in my shoulder, I could hear something familiar in those voices. I closed my eyes and tried to listen, but all I could think about was the pain. Part of me wanted to sleep and part of me wanted to listen to what the voices were saying, but most of me simply wanted the pain to quit. I opened my eyes again.

The pain was rising and falling like an ocean tide and I caught the pain going out and could see that I was lying in a shallow depression on the bank, a place the water had gouged out, I suppose, overgrown with Queen Anne's Lace, Johnson grass, and cattails. Higher up the bank there were wild daisies and Russian thistles. Birds chirped in the trees above me and the stench of stagnant water stained the air. Frogs were starting up around me and the light was going fast now. Close to the water it was already dusky.

The pain eased for a moment and I could make out who the voices belonged to. Taking a deep breath, I tried to think. Gladys and Johnny were somewhere close. Perhaps just on the other side of the bramble thicket off to my left. If I couldn't see them, I reasoned, then they couldn't see me. The trunk of a large sycamore was maybe three feet away and I tried to squirm closer. If I could get there and get my back up against that trunk, they'd have the devil's own time spotting me in the twilight. I glanced skyward. Fifteen minutes, maybe twenty, and I'd be nothing more than another shadow. Maybe I could get out of this yet. If I didn't bleed to death first. Moving as quietly as I could, I pulled a fairly clean, if damp, handkerchief out of my back pocket and pressed it gently against the bullet hole. My shoulder hurt like hell, but I couldn't feel a bullet working around inside of me. My arm felt kind of numb, but I didn't think the bullet had hit any bones.

"Johnny?"

"What?"

"How bad hurt you reckon he is?" To my ears, Gladys sounded anxious. If I were in her shoes, I probably would have been anxious, too. I kept squirming. The bleeding had started again, but I didn't see how I had any choice but to keep moving.

"I don't know," Johnny said. "Bullet must have tore a hunk out of him. He left a lot of blood back there."

"Wonder if he's he still bleeding?"

"Hard to say. He must have got it stopped somehow, or else we've lost the trail. Probably spent too much time checking out that river bank, but I swear I heard him splashing in the water. Didn't realize the light would go so fast. In amongst these trees, night falls in a hurry."

"Reckon he's dead?"

"Don't know, but he's hurt bad for sure. If he don't get some doctoring soon I'd say he's a goner. Which I guess would please you sure enough."

"Yes, it would. You have no idea how tired I got pretending to care."

"Ray wasn't such a bad guy."

"You never had to make love to him. He was boring. Never really made me feel alive."

"Can't speak to that, for sure, but he and I sure had some times together. Covered a lot of miles. Had each other's back for better than three years. Plenty of times he's pulled me out of a jam. That's why I couldn't make myself pull the trigger."

"I wondered what the trouble was. Figured you was about gutless."

"Hey now."

"Oh, shut up. You'd best shut up and get down there and see if you can find him. Surely you can find a man who's been shot."

"Gladys, it's getting too dark to see, especially down in that underbrush. It's already dark enough down there that I could walk within three feet of him and never even know he was close by. Besides, he won't last long. We should be making tracks before somebody notices the car and starts asking questions."

"How do you figure he won't last long? One thing I know for sure is that Ray is a stubborn son-of-a-bitch. What makes you think he is just going to lay down and die?"

"Infection, silly. Bullet wound always needs washing out good. Antiseptic for sure. Maybe Ray got the bleeding stopped, but that don't mean much. Usually, it's not the bullet that kills a man, but the infection that comes after. Ray needs to be in a hospital, or at least see a doctor."

"But we can't take a chance. You never know. Some old farmer might come along and find him and play Good Samaritan."

"I know," Johnny said. "I know."

"What are you going to do?" I pictured her standing there at the top of the rise with her fists on her hips. "Well, what are we going to do about him?" Her voice sounded hard to me. Hard like a closed fist.

"I don't know," Johnny said, "I purely don't know."

"We've got to get moving, Johnny, like you said. Police will be hunting hard for us everywhere. Let's backtrack and see if he's trying to slip around behind us. Losing all that blood he can't have gone far. For sure, it'll be dark in less than half an hour. If we don't find him by then, we'll have to move on, and hope. You've got me bad worried about the law now."

"Well, we are across the state line."

"You sure?"

"Sure, I'm sure," Johnny said. "Saw the welcome to Louisiana sign about two miles back."

"But won't they be looking for us on account of that other bank job?"

"Hadn't thought of that."

My shoulder was throbbing like something alive. I closed my eyes against the pain.

"Johnny?"

"What?"

"Won't they be looking for three people?"

"Suppose so. Three, or four if they never found Donald."

"But there will be just two of us, see."

"What are you driving at, Gladys?"

"I'll tell you what I'm driving at, you big dummy. If we'd gone driving all over Louisiana with Ray, they'd have caught us sure. But being just two of us and we got a chance. A good chance. We can be a married couple, see? Man and wife. On our honeymoon, see?"

"I see all right, but what about Ray? What if he ain't dead and the law finds him?"

I held my breath, waiting for Gladys to say something. I was deep in the shadows now and all the light was dying. That was good, 'cause I didn't see how I could go another foot. Frogs croaked behind me and something splashed the surface of the water. The sun had gone down all the way and the afterlight was all that was left. But I could see clear how stupid I'd been to ignore those little glances they didn't think I saw, those touches, those sudden silences when I'd come in a room. I let out my breath and tried to think.

"Don't talk crazy, honey."

"But, Gladys."

"This is our big chance, Johnny. One good chance at making a decent life for ourselves. All that money, honey. All that nice green money will buy us a ticket to paradise. Now, I know Ray is a good man. In fact, I know that better than anybody. But he's boring and a stick-in-the-mud and now he's shot up bad. But we can't just leave him and go on. If he's alive, we can't never make a new life for ourselves. This is our one big chance. We've got real money, and we'll probably never have this much again, and you know it. This is it, Johnny baby, our one true chance. Now, you know I love you, so go on down there and take care of things so we don't have to never worry again. For me, baby, do it for me. For me, and for us."

"All right, Gladys, I'll go. You circle back. But I don't think we can find him today, not with daylight going down like the Titanic. If we can't find him, we'll have to hole up somewhere close and keep hunting until we track him down, or find his body. If we don't, we'd never draw a peaceful breath, and you know that. I recognize this is our big chance, but, like you said, we can't leave Ray behind. Not alive, we can't. Not alive."

"All right, baby, go on down and I'll circle back. But if you see him again, don't hesitate. Promise me?"

I lay motionless, hardly breathing at all, feeling the pain running through me and waiting on Johnny to say something. I could hear the frogs and the birds and smell stagnant water and damp earth and my own blood, and I knew that if something didn't change soon, I was going to die on a creek bank alongside a back road in Louisiana.

I tried moving my legs. They worked now, after a fashion. My right arm felt okay and my head was clearing. Except for the fire burning my left arm I was as good as ever. Ha, what a joke. What did they call joking at a time like this? Oh yes, gallows humor.

"All right, already," Johnny said, "all right, I'll go down there and take care of things. No hesitating this time."

"Aw baby, I knew you'd come through for us. Give me a kiss."

I wanted to vomit and I wanted to cry. But I didn't do either one. Didn't even stick around for their lousy kiss. Instead, I started scooting on my good side, heading down toward the bulrushes and the murmuring water and the frogs. Darkness was falling all around like black rain, and that sweet blackness was my only hope. Not that I had a plan. Keep moving and start praying was about all I could do. But then my left arm was throbbing like it was falling off and I hadn't believed in God since I was a kid.

Closer to the water, it was muddy going, and by working my legs back and forth, I could move along better than I'd figured I would. Then I was sliding into the water and when the water hit the bullet hole I gasped and my head swirled like some carnival ride. Somehow, I got over on my good side and sorta floated along, kicking softly when I could, praying a little when I remembered.

Fourteen

I COULD HEAR a buzzing. I was roasting alive and I could hear a buzzing. My shoulder throbbed and waves of pain rippled across my brain.

My brain felt so hot that I thought it surely must be melting. My body ached like I'd been tromped on by a horse. My shoulder hurt so bad I wanted to cry, but real men don't cry. Biting my lip, I rolled over.

I was lying on the ground. That much I'd figured out. After a couple of false tries, I blinked my eyes open. I was afraid of what I'd see, but all I could see was a pale blue sky, with clouds spotted across it like cotton balls flung by a giant.

Turning my head, I could see that I was lying in a field. Grass and weeds covered the ground and the smell of manure was strong and fresh as though cattle had been in the field recently. Then I heard something heavy clomping toward me and I turned and stared up into the face of a Jersey cow. Milked enough of them in Missouri to know what one looked like.

That flash of thought brought back the day before and I knew why, my shoulder felt like it was being ripped apart. Waving my hand at the cow, I tried to sit up. On the third try I made it. The day had been alive only a short time. The sun still hung low in the east. Already, though, there was heat in that light. My brain felt thick, full of sludge. I could vaguely remember stumbling up an embankment along what looked like a cow path.

I was sitting in an overgrown pasture. Bees were buzzing around the patch of red clover I'd been lying in. Although I couldn't clearly remember how I'd gotten there, judging from the shape my trousers were in, I must have crawled most of the way. They were caked with mud, and damp, as though I'd gone swimming in them. Then I remembered the sluggish river and knew I couldn't sit in the middle of a field with a herd of milk cows. I began to try and get my legs under me.

By the time I was standing, sweat was rolling and I could feel blood trickling down my chest. My legs were trembling and felt a long way away. All I wanted was to find a nice soft bed and lie down. But for damn sure that wasn't in the cards. Even with my sludge filled brain I knew that. I started walking. The pasture sloped upwards.

I tried to go up the slope, figuring once I got up on top I might find a road. At least I could see more of the country. Down in the grassy depression I couldn't get my bearings. Once I got started I found out damn quick how weak I was. If I took it easy, I could walk some, but going uphill was beyond me.

I began walking along the side of slope. Ten steps later, I could see what appeared to be a cow path weaving its way south. At the end of the meadow were trees, second-growth locust and cedars with a lot of undergrowth. The wind shifted and for a second I could smell stagnant water and wondered if I was only going back the way I'd come. Part of me figured it would be smart to stop and try to sort things out, but the rest of me knew that if I sat down again, I might not ever get up. By the time I made the timber, the sun was climbing the sky and the heat was rising. My shoulder ached like hell and my legs weren't working worth a damn. Still, I was glad to get out of the sun.

There was a tradeoff for the shade, however. Brambles grew under the spindly trees and bushes and vines grabbed at me like green snakes. Real snakes probably crawled in there, too, but I couldn't worry about that now. A couple of two-legged snakes were my true concern. I'd wandered off the cow path and couldn't find it; my head was starting to ache and my brain felt hot and fuzzy, like I was coming down with a fever. Fevers, I knew.

Spots slow-danced before my eyes. Little squiggly shapes that floated like so many dust motes. Mosquitoes whined in my ears and bit me anywhere they could find skin. I tried to find a way to hold my shoulder that wouldn't hurt, but it kept throbbing. A vine caught my shoe and I stumbled forward into a black locust tree. Leaning against the trunk, I closed my eyes and tried to think.

The pain wasn't easing, though, and when I put my right palm against my forehead it felt unnaturally hot. All I wanted was to sit down for five minutes, but had enough mind left to know that those five minutes might well be my death warrant, and I sure as hell didn't want to die in some second-rate Louisiana jungle. I pushed off that tree and started moving again.

When I'd been a kid, one of my uncles had been a fiend about the Civil War. Instead of talking about the weather or baseball or women, he always seemed to steer the conversation to Grant and Billy Sherman and Pap Thomas. or Lee and Stonewall Jackson. Them, and A.P. Hill and Longstreet and P.G.T. Beauregard and Pickett's Charge. I'd heard all his stories a dozen times. One of them came back to me. It was about a battle, in Virginia, I think, called The Wilderness. The Wilderness, from the way my uncle told it, must have been about like what I was stumbling through, brambles and vines and scrub timber full of dead limbs and unhealthy air, and then the whole place catching fire and the smoke growing so thick the Confederates and the Union men couldn't see one another until they ran headlong into each other. He told about men groaning in pain and crying out for water, and their mothers, and, when the end was near, God. Guess it was about as bad as it gets. Anyway, I remembered that story and wished my uncle was there with me, 'cause this was sure enough a damn nasty hole and I was shot just as bad as if I'd been one of Bobby Lee's Virginians.

Beneath the trees it was dark, and the humidity was awful. The air was thick with flies, mosquitoes, and all sorts of strange bugs. Once, a snake slithered across an opening in front of me, every bit as thick as my forearm. Damp air stank of rot and decay and death. Hell all right, and I was going to die in it if I didn't keep moving.

Amongst the trees, I'd lost sight of the sun, and without it, any sense of time. Might have been noon or mid-afternoon, or going on for dark. The fever had me now, smoldering like a banked fire in my brain. My arm was aching so bad I'd sure enough have let a doctor amputate.

But there weren't any doctors and I had no idea where I was, or even what direction I was moving. The one comfort about this wildness was that even if Gladys and Johnny were still searching, they'd play hell finding me. More likely, by now they figured I'd died from loss of blood, or shock. Or maybe they thought I'd drowned. I didn't give a damn about them or what they thought. Everything had become as clear as new-blown glass.

I didn't try to think any more. Or maybe I simply couldn't. Once, I fell, or rather my legs gave way. For a long while I lay with one side of my face in the damp earth and the mosquitoes and black flies crawling all over me. Kept telling myself to get up, though, and finally made it to one knee. After resting some more, I made it all the way to erect. Then I started moving again.

You couldn't truly call what I was doing walking. Lurching or staggering was more like it. Ever few steps, my brain got to where it wasn't thinking at all. Then I'd come back into myself real sudden like, no more knowing what I'd been doing than if I was a gopher. Like sleep walking, only I wasn't asleep. Maybe I was more like those zombies some coloreds worshipped.

I couldn't tell whether I was going in one direction or circles now and I started seeing things. Visions. Faces mostly, like my dad's and mom's, then the old man who batched on the next farm north of us. Finally, I saw Joker, a dog I'd had when I was a kid. Joker had been a good dog. Lived to seventeen, my dad told me years later. When I'd heard that dog had died, I sure enough cried.

By now my head was spinning like I was drunk, and when I saw Gladys and Johnny standing there in front of me, I liked to screamed and vomited at the same time.

Only it wasn't them, only a couple of saplings that had intertwined; I felt like laughing at myself. Only laughing was simply too much trouble.

A jaybird started screeching at me and he kept on until I looked up to try to find him. Never saw him though, 'cause when I twisted my neck and lifted my head it somehow made the earth start spinning until it felt as if I was inside a barrel rolling downhill.

Everything started going black and kept going until there was only a tiny pinprick of light. It took me a while, but I finally figured out that light was my pain, and that it was the last light in the world. Then that final light flickered and went out, and I was falling, falling, falling.

Fifteen

I COULD FEEL my mind crawling out of something more than sleep and less than death. Wasn't sure whether I wanted it to keep crawling or not. Had that feeling you get when you're coming out of deep sleep and you're not quite awake, yet you're alert enough to recognize you're not fully in this world, or the next. Hot light bathed my face. My face felt coated with sweat and I wondered where I was. Then I shifted position, felt the pain, and knew. I opened my eyes.

I was sitting with my back against a tree stump. A field of horseweeds, milkweeds, and rabbit tobacco spread out before me, sloping down to a dark river. Taking a longer look, I could see that the coffee-colored water was barely moving. More of a slough, say, or bayou.

Heat waves shimmered between me and the water. A bird called out from the tree line along the far bank. The call was foreign to me. Idly, I wondered what the bird looked like, but I didn't move. My body felt tired, washed out, and my shoulder was throbbing again. I let my eyes drift down to the pain. The piece of shirt I'd stuffed in the wound had been soaked through, but the bleeding seemed to have stopped, at least for the moment.

While the fever was down, I needed to get up and move, but my legs felt the way cooked spaghetti looks. I hadn't had water or food in better than a day, and if I didn't get help soon, I was a goner. I knew that, but didn't see how I could ever find help in the ass-end of civilization. In a way, I was surprised I'd come so far. At least I'd made it out of the wilderness. For some unknown reason I felt proud of that.

Guess I faded off again, because when the strange bird started up again, I jerked and came back into the day, only more alert this time. If I hadn't heard laughter right then maybe I'd have simply sat where I was and bled to death, or died of the fever that was burning in me, or simply rotted away like an old oak. But laughter drifted to me from near the water and I made up my mind to get off my butt and go see if I could get some help.

It took me a couple of tries to even get to standing. The water sounded distant and I wanted to sit back down. My legs were trembling, but I told myself I was going downhill and could make it. A dying man will tell himself anything. One step was an effort, but I took another, and then another.

By the time I made the willows that lined the bank, every inch of my body was soaked with sweat and I'd started bleeding again. Blood felt warm and sticky trickling down my chest, and I knew in my gut that if it kept on flowing I wasn't going to make it.

Inside the willows, the air was close and still, but the leaves cut the sunlight considerable. Glad to get out of the sun, I leaned against the largest trunk, pressed a hand across the hole in my shoulder, and listened. For a moment I thought I must have imagined the laughter; then I heard it again, followed by a low murmur of voices. I pushed off the tree, hurrying now, because my head was starting to spin and my hand was soaked with blood.

On the bank the ground was slick and I slipped and would have gone down, except I fell against a sycamore trunk and hung on until I got my balance back. Taking a deep breath, I started moving again. Each stumbling step was painful and I tried to take them carefully. If I went down again, I'd never get up. Life gets simple like that sometimes.

How long I staggered along that riverbank I couldn't say. While I was still inside the trees, I was better off, because I could stop and lean against one if I had to. But they thinned out until they quit in a bend of the slough or bayou or whatever it was, and that was that.

Except for a few clumps of grass and a log that washed up in the last high water, the bank was bare. The voices had died off and I wanted to cry. But crying never helped anybody and I'd be damned if I was going to cry now. Not after what all I had gone through. Besides, I aimed to settle a score. Putting my head down, I kept moving. I could smell leaves rotting in the water and my sweat and blood; then I could smell something else. For a minute I couldn't place the scent, but in a bit it came to me. Fried meat.

Maybe I was dreaming, but that didn't matter much, considering. All I could do was keep putting one foot in front of another, hanging close to the water, trying to listen for the voices above my labored breathing. But they had vanished. Never had my legs felt this tired.

I was going to die along this lousy backwater.

Dead in Louisiana and not a person who knew or cared about me within three hundred miles. No, that wasn't quite right. Johnny and Gladys would be hanging close, and they sure cared about me, all right. Cared a helluva lot if I was dead or alive.

Dying was an aspect of life I'd never given much thought to, but I'd always counted on there being someone to say a few words over me. Pray for my departing soul, that sort of thing. Seemed like only frogs, mosquitoes, and horse flies were going to witness my demise.

Sure, those were morbid thoughts, but at least they helped keep my mind off the pain. The shoulder kept throbbing, though, and the fever was rising and I wasn't seeing good anymore. All I could think about was lying down on that cool, hard-packed, bare earth and resting awhile. Just a little while.

Ten more steps, I told myself; ten more steps and you can rest. I made the ten and argued for ten more. Each one was harder to take. Felt like I was trying to walk through cooling molasses. Twenty yards ahead, the river bent back to the south and I told myself to make the bend and that would be it, no matter what. For once I was telling myself the truth.

Halfway there I wouldn't have bet a buffalo nickel I was going to make it, but I summoned up a pinch of pride and kept putting one foot in front of another. For a few steps, I imagined I was Cortez, or one of those Spanish Conquistadors I'd read about in school. Then my mind drifted and I came back inside myself; I was deep in the bend. My head was swimming and the ground seemed to slant sideways, but I was coming out of the slickened earth and craving rest. Live or die, I was going to lie down. God, if He was still around, could save me, or not. Up to Him. I was beyond caring.

All of a sudden the river straightened out and I quit walking. My body was swaying and I glanced at the ground. Three steps ahead was a patch of grass that looked green and soft, and without thinking much I headed for it. My arm throbbed worse than ever and I heard myself groan.

At first I thought it was a mirage. I blinked and the picture cleared, then went blurry again. I rubbed at my eyes with my good hand and peered through the sun and shadows.

Three people were sitting on the river bank, cane poles jammed in the soft ground, their faces turned toward me. Their skin was black and shining, like fresh washed coal. Had I passed on without knowing it? And if I had, where in the name of all that was good and holy had I ended up?

I felt faint. My head was very heavy. My legs simply refused to move anymore. The patch of grass was only a step away. Told myself I could make that. Told myself I was seeing visions. Without any intention my eyes closed and my knees buckled. The earth rose to meet me.

Sixteen

BABOON FACES STARED down at me. Back in my younger days, I'd seen baboons in the St. Louis Zoo and I wondered how I'd gotten back to that place. Then I could feel pain and knew I wasn't at any zoo.

Baboon voices murmured above me. Baboons couldn't talk, but these were talking. I studied on that some. The only answer I could come up with was I was out of my mind with fever.

My shoulder burned and my head ached and I could feel my pulse throbbing down the side of my throat. I tried to get up, but my legs weren't working anymore. I heard myself groan. The sound was faint and seemed to come from far away. Sweat rolled down into my eyes and I blinked against the stinging.

"No sir, that man ain't dead," a voice said. The voice sound young, like it belonged to a kid. Really, it was more drawled sounds than speech, and the vowels were thick and slurred.

"Ah," said an even younger sounding voice, "thought for sure that man was dead. But still, he ain't moving much.

Maybe we ought to go through his pockets. For identification and sech, see."

"Ah, you igno, you can't do no sech a thing. That'd be like robbing the dead."

"But he ain't dead."

"No, but he may soon will be."

I wanted to speak up and tell them that I wasn't going to die, that I only needed a little help. But my lips weren't working right and baboons or gorilla or whatever they were wouldn't understand me anyway. So how could I understand them? I was bad confused. Fever crazed, without a doubt.

"What you boys doing?"

"Nothing, Mama."

"Only looking at a dead man is all."

"What you mean, looking at a dead man? Quit your fooling, Leroy, and get back over here."

"Leroy ain't fooling, Mama. There is a man over here, but he ain't dead, only bad hurt."

"What you mean, bad hurt? Fool's probably drunk."

"No, no, Mama, he's bleeding and everything. Think he's done got shot."

"Tyree, you ain't storying to me now, are you?"

"No, Mama."

"Is it one of them Williams boys? They's always getting in fights. Bet it's Durcel."

"No, it ain't Durcel. I know him and this sure ain't him. You ain't gonna believe this Mama, but this here man is a white man."

"Oh, sweet Jesus, my sweet Jesus, a white man. Tyree, Leroy, you boys know that white man's face?"

"Ain't never seen him, neither of us."

I could hear the woman talking some more and I wanted to call out to her, but my mind was on fire and everything was going dark.

Then all I could feel was the pain.

Then I was floating.

Seventeen

SOMETHING WET WAS swiping my face. My skin felt hot and the cool wetness was welcome. Again, I tried again to open my eyes and this time they came open and I could see clearly. Well, more clearly.

It wasn't baboons at all. Just a big, fat colored woman and two young colored boys. A mammy and two pickaninnies. What lousy luck. I couldn't catch a break.

The woman was washing my face with a rag that smelled like it had been pulled out of a bucket of stagnant water. Probably had been dunked in the damn slough, or swamp, or whatever the hell it was. Still, the water felt good against my face. Cool. My skin felt like it was glowing the way metal still glows even after you pull it out of the fire.

"You got your eyes open. Well now, that's a good sign. I sure enough don't know you, mister. Tell the truth, don't believe I've laid eyes on you afore. You from around here?"

I licked my lips and a trickle of water ran into my mouth. It tasted like pond water, but I was so thirsty that I was grateful. "No," I croaked. "Got lost."

"Well, I figured you wasn't no Robicheaux Parish man. Colored and white, guess I know most everybody living here, and lots that's gone on. My name is Vivian Washburn."

I didn't tell her my name. Wasn't no use in her knowing it. Soon as I could get to civilization and white men and a doctor, I wouldn't have any use for her. None at all.

"Well, that's all right, mister. You save your breath and your strength. I can see you done been through a terrible bad time. Appears like you might have got shot. You have an accident?"

"Yeah," I said, "I shot myself." Telling that lie didn't bother me. Not to a fat black mammy. No need for anyone to know too much. I was in a bad jam and the less other people knew about me the better. If this woman could get me to town, I just might be able to pull myself out of the quicksand.

"Figured a bullet made that hole. Patched you up best as I could with a swatch offen one of my clean dresses. Bleeding's eased off considerable, but that wound needs tending to proper. A nice washing would maybe do you a lot of good."

"Got a car?" I asked.

Her big eyes opened wide and she shook her head.

"How about a wagon?"

"No, sir. Ain't got no car nor no wagon. Since old Henry died last fall, don't even have a mule. Only animals on the place are a few chickens, a three-legged dog, and a cat that comes and goes as he pleases."

What the hell did I care about livestock? The fever was rising again and I knew I had to talk fast.

"What I need is a doctor. Know of one close by?"

She closed her African eyes and I could almost see her brain working. About as bright as that mule that died, I figured. Groaning, I eased into a sitting position.

"No, sir, closest doctor is clear over to Broughton. And that's pert near twelve miles as the crow flies. Twenty by road, I'd judge."

I took a deep breath. I wanted to curse her till a fly wouldn't light on her, but I was in a bind. Being helpless like this purely galled me. More so since it was a dumb colored woman I was dependent on. I studied her face—it was the color of the blackest shoe polish, only the polish needed buffing. Her lips were three times as fat as Gladys'. Merely looking at her disgusted me. But, as my Uncle George used to say, I was between a rock and a hard spot—and both were jabbing me.

"Know anybody that's got a pickup or a wagon?"

"No, mister, I sure don't. Oh, people in town have such, and, of course, some rich farmers over toward Bradfordsville. But all the people I know are strictly from poverty. Moses Ellis, he's got a mule, and Tom Upton, why he got a swayback old horse, but they four, five miles away and no telling if they home, or out working, or off on a drinking spree somewhere."

"Damn it, Mammy, shut up talking and listen. I need a doctor. Can you get one for me, or not?"

She shook her head and the fat in her cheeks wobbled. She was the blackest colored I'd seen since that juke joint. That night seemed weeks ago. Almost like another man had inhabited my body then. I glanced at the woman again. When the sunlight struck her just right, her skin took on a purple hue—the color of a ripe eggplant.

"Can't you see plain I need a doctor? How stupid are you?"

"Now, mister, there's no need to get yourself all worked up. You're a sick man. I can see the fever rising in you like you was the thermometer outside Pascal's Drug Store."

Had to give the darky that one. The fever sure enough had a grip on my brain. Felt like it was going to sizzle any minute. The pain from the bullet had eased some. I'd heard some mammies was dang good at doctoring the sick and afflicted. Well, that was all right with me, as long as they stuck to their own kind. Bothered me to know that she'd been touching me, and worse, that the hem of her dress was touching my bare skin. I hoped I didn't catch some nasty disease. Felt like I ought to say something, but talking suddenly seemed too much of an effort. I could feel those three coloreds staring at me, which made me nervous. I shook my head, trying to clear the fog out of my brain.

"Go away," I croaked.

"What? And leave you here all by your lonesome in such a condition? No sir, I couldn't do that. No way. Why that would go hard against my religion. Bible teaches plain that we must be our brother's keeper. Perhaps you've read the parable of the Good Samaritan?"

"To hell with your religion." I swung my right arm at her. It seemed very heavy and moved extraordinarily slowly. She leaned back and I could feel myself falling, toppling like a jar sliding off the edge of a shelf. My face smacked against the earth and pain shot through my shoulder. My head whirled like a globe spun by a giant. Everything went dark. Then I could see the light again and feel hands touching me.

"Here now, Tyree, you get ahold of his good arm and I'll try to lift here below where the bullet went in."

"Quit," I said, but the word came out kind of squashed.

"Yes, Mama."

"No," I tried to say, but all that came out of my mouth was a moan. I felt old and tired. In the course of a day, I had aged to ninety. At least I sure enough felt like it.

"I can help, too." The voice was high and squeaky and seemed to come for a long way away. Those hands had a good grip on me now and I knew they wanted me to stand. Only, I didn't want to. Maybe I should, I thought, but I didn't want to. I could feel the hands pulling on me. After a while it seemed like less trouble to try and stand up than to fight it. I gathered up what strength I still had and tried to get off the ground.

All the strength seemed to have gone out of my legs. I told myself I could stand up. I told myself I could do anything. But that was all a lie. If it hadn't been for those hands holding on and tugging and pulling, I'd have fallen again. I could hear the voices, chattering like monkeys, but I couldn't understand the words. The ground seemed to gently rise and fall, like I was standing on an ocean.

They were tugging on me, urging me to do something. I tried to understand, but their words were nothing more than the humming of a hive of bees. Gradually, I began to sense that they wanted me to walk. Merely thinking about walking made me tired, but finally it seemed maybe I ought to try and walk instead of standing there swaying like a flagpole. I took one step, then another.

I could feel their hands on me. When I was a kid, my mother's sister, who was real religious, took me to church with her a few times. At her church they believed in the laying on of hands. That what those colored hands felt like on me – exactly like they were laying hands on me, praying for me, for my soul.

Imagine that, coloreds practicing the laying on of hands on me. Me a pure-bred white man. Made me sick at my stomach. Worse, there wasn't a damn thing I could do about it. I was shot up bad and had lost what felt like a bucket of blood. But the fever was the worst. A man might die from a gunshot, sure, but he could also push through pain. At least that was what I believed. Fever, though, robbed a man of his strength, and his courage.

We kept moving. I don't know how, but I kept swinging one foot in front of the other and that Black mother and those two colored boys kept me upright. The sun had shifted and we kept moving into and out of shadows. It seemed like we had walked for two days.

I wanted to sit down, but the voice at the back of my brain kept telling me to keep moving. Once, when were in a thicket of tall trees, we paused for a moment and the biggest boy held a Mason jar to my lips. It was partly full of water. The water was lukewarm and tasted oily, but I drank it. After that, we started walking again, moving beneath trees that towered above us. In the shelter of their leaves, the air was cooler and I felt a touch better.

For a few minutes we made decent progress. Then the fever started to rise again and I guess I purely went out of my head. Kept seeing faces of people who'd been dead for years. Only their faces weren't right. Maybe their eyes and nose were mixed up, or they didn't have any ears at all. Then I saw the faces of Johnny and Gladys.

They were directly in front of me, staring straight into my eyes, close enough that I could smell the stench of their bodies and feel the heat of their breath on my face. Without asking, I knew why they had come. They had come to finish what they started. They had come to kill me.

To hell with them. Let them kill me. I didn't care. I truly didn't care anymore. I closed my eyes and waited for the bullet. In one way, that would be a blessing. At least I wouldn't be in pain anymore, and I wouldn't have to be handled by coloreds.

I waited what seemed like a long time. Nothing happened. Maybe I was already dead? I forced my eyes open. Gladys and Johnny were still there, their faces huge like the moon can be when it first starts to rise.

“Kill me,” I said. “Go ahead and kill me.”

They were grinning. Their faces were pumpkins carved at Halloween. Then, as I stared at them, waiting for the bullet with my name on it, their faces grew long and thin and yellow. Then they began to melt.

Eighteen

I WAS IN A NEW LAND, a land of fevers and dreams. By turns I soaked myself with sweat and chilled like the ague had settled forever in my bones. I dreamed of people I'd known, living and dead, people with tails and horns, people with arms and legs that looked as if they'd been twisted by a tornado. Funny thing was, all the people in my dreams had black faces.

At times I could feel myself rising toward what seemed like the surface. For a long time, I thought I had been swimming and a cramp had pulled me down to the bottom of a deep lake and now I was rising, slowly floating toward the surface. But I guess it wasn't a watery surface I was trying to reach; it was simply to come back to consciousness.

There were days I thought I heard voices, and once I'm sure I heard thunder rolling. But most of the time I lay in a stupor, sweating in a miserable heat, trying to crawl back inside my mind. Pain radiated from my left shoulder and I was vaguely aware of people touching me, pressing soft cloths against my body.

Guess my mind must have been drifting. Kept remembering back when I was a kid, or when Johnny and I first hooked up and began the life. Times seemed better then. Soft light illuminated those memories and a sweet fragrance drifted about them. Only they tumbled out broken up and jumbled, out of order, the way pieces of a jigsaw puzzle scatter on the table when you dump them from the box.

One memory that kept drifting to the surface was when I was a kid and wanted a pony of my own more than anything in the world. But I never got that pony. The only stock Dad had on the place were a few sheep, a milk cow, some chickens, and a stray mutt or two, including one he called Fireball for some reason nobody ever figured out.

I thought, too, about women I'd known. But most of my thoughts were about me and Johnny and how things were good when we started out. In those days we were straight from starvation, and so was just about everybody else, except a few bankers and railroad magnets. Seemed like if a man was poor, he was a whole lot more likely to do you a favor than if he had a pocket full of money.

Seeing a few with so much money didn't sit right with me or Johnny. We didn't want to be rich ourselves, only make enough to get by on, enough for each of us to support a wife and a couple of kids and have a decent car to drive. Hoover had promised a chicken in every pot, but when the hard times came, America found out his promise was only wind.

In the early days we'd have worked – taken about any job that was available. Least ways anything where a man could keep his feet on the ground. I'd seen pictures in the papers about men in Chicago and New York working ten, fifteen, twenty stories up off the ground, building what the writers called skyscrapers. Don't know about scraping the sky—that would be going some—but anything over ten feet off the ground was too high for me.

Johnny and me, we'd both worked dozens of odd jobs, digging ditches and graves, carrying beef carcasses at Armour and Swift, digging potatoes, working on railroad tracks. If it was a job that paid, why we'd run to be first in line. Later, I'd think back many a night about those days and how working and living honest made a man feel good.

But nothing good ever lasts. Least it never has for me, and not for most poor folks. 'Course what happened was the jobs dried up and the government wasn't doing a blessed thing to help. Plus, standing in a long line of dirty, hungry men just to get a bowl of watery soup and a crust of dry bread wore thin quick. There was talk of Roosevelt and a New Deal, but an empty stomach can't wait.

After a time, me and Johnny got other ideas. Maybe they weren't all strictly legal, but they weren't real bad ones either. Not the way we saw the world then.

All we'd ever aimed to do was rob a few banks. Get back some of what those rich bankers had stolen from others. Lots of times, 'specially at first, Johnny and I had given away most of what we got in the robbery. Why, one time over in Illinois, maybe two miles outside Metropolis, our car had started overheating and we'd pulled off and driven down a gravel lane to an old farmhouse. When the farmer had come out to see what we wanted, we'd gotten to talking and, after we'd hauled up a couple of buckets from the well and got the radiator filled back up, he'd asked us inside to have some supper with him and his wife.

Cornbread and a bowl of beans was it, but we hadn't eaten all day and that cornbread and beans tasted like that milk and honey preachers talk about. While we were eating, we got to talking about how hard the times were all over, and the old farmer, he had to be seventy, told us that if he didn't make a payment soon he was going to lose the place to the Bank of Metropolis. Said that farm had been in his family for way over a hundred years and he sure did hate to lose it, but he and the old lady didn't have a dime cash money between them.

His wife didn't talk much, but she kept dabbing at her eyes and sniffing now and then, so I knew that she hated like everything to lose the place, especially her furniture and keepsakes. Those were the early days of Hoover's Depression, and Johnny and I were a pair of young bucks forged steel tough by the Depression and could get by on a mouthful of gravel and a gob of spit. So, can't say I was much surprised when Johnny stood up and dug a fifty-dollar bill and a handful of coins out of his trousers and tossed them on the table and told the old man to go down to the bank in the morning and make a payment and tell those bankers to kiss his overalls.

I didn't say much, 'cause the old woman had started in to crying, but I added a few bills to Johnny's fifty, and maybe everybody's eyes got a little moist. Like I said, we were younger in those times, and hadn't seen all the mean things people do to one another.

Dreams of those days filled my days and nights. Dreams of seeing people in coffins, and dogs that had been struck by cars lying in the road with their eyes open and guts hanging out, and women with golden hair and two faces. Pretty sure I cried out a few times. Could hear myself screaming, only I was such a long way away that my own voice came to me only as an echo.

How long I lay like that I can't say. Most of the time I was completely out of my head. Now and then I'd float toward that surface, but I'd never quite reach the air on the other side, and in a few minutes I'd start to sink. Got to be a pattern, rising and falling back, never quite making the free air. Rising and falling, rising and falling, rising...

Nineteen

It was evening—I could tell by the quality of the light—and a breeze was blowing. Moving air felt cool against my cheek, and a sweet scent, like honeysuckle in bloom, swirled through it. For a moment I was still a boy, living on the homeplace back in Missouri. Then I shifted positions and pain burnt through me like heat from a branding iron and I knew right enough where I was.

I sat up careful and watched the room spin. When the spinning slowed, I could see that the place was nothing more than a cabin with rough lumber walls and a smooth-packed earthen floor. A small table was pushed against one wall and three chairs stood around it.

At the end of the room was a stove. Above the stove, three shelves were nailed into the walls. Jars and a few cans stood on the shelves. In one corner, a board had been laid across two buckets, and on the board were sacks that looked like they might hold meal or flour. One window provided the only light in the cabin. An oil lamp stood on the table, but it wasn't lit. Two pictures—they looked like they'd been cut out of magazines—were nailed to opposite walls. One was of a white Jesus, the other of President Franklin D. Roosevelt. The cabin smelled of dirt, fried meat, and stale sweat. I swung my legs around slowly and eased toward the floor.

Bare earth felt cool against the bottom of my feet and I sat there for a minute, getting my balance and listening to birds chirping outside the cabin. I wasn't wearing a shirt and my shoulder was bandaged with what appeared to be clean rags knotted together. I was thirsty and lightheaded at the same time. A cigarette sure would have tasted fine. I took a deep breath and stood up.

At least I tried to stand. All my strength seemed to have evaporated. My legs were as limber as young cornstalks. I sat back down on the bed and rested. While I rested, I thought about what I needed to do. Didn't take long to remember the fat colored woman and the two jabbering boys. Figured I must be in their cabin; for sure, I was in a predicament.

First thing was to get dressed and get the hell out. Thank God, I still had my pants on. No telling what diseases I'd have caught lying naked in one of their beds.

The bed wasn't much, simply a homemade job big enough for one person and shoved against a wall. No way that fat mammy and two growing boys could sleep in this bed. I looked around for another. There wasn't one I could see, but it appeared there might be another room off the kitchen. The light was starting to go, though, and I couldn't be certain. I stood again.

My legs were still trembly, but the blood was flowing better and I took a cautious step and got a hand on the wall. The room was holding still, and I shuffled to the door.

It wasn't quite as late in the day as it had seemed because the cabin was set inside a natural circle of live oaks. A few locust and black oak were mixed in and the sun had gone down behind them. What light filtered through the trees was feeble.

I looked around for the others. At first, all I could see was trees and a streak of bare earth, with a line strung between two trees running above it. Dresses and overalls were hanging from the line. Then I noticed a break in the trees and spotted a splash of color. It was moving rhythmically, maybe thirty yards away. I leaned against the doorframe, wondering if I could walk that far. After a bit I decided maybe I could. I pushed off the doorframe and started for that moving swatch of color.

My legs were so weak and trembly I thought sure I'd collapse in the dirt. I wondered how long it had been since I'd eaten. Movement seemed to bring a little strength up from somewhere and I made it across the clearing. Among the trees it was better. They were huge old trees with branches bigger around than my waist and it was pleasant to feel their certain strength when I rested against one for a moment. I wondered how old they were. Judging by their size they had to have been here a while. Maybe as long ago as when Indians and alligators roamed the territory.

Rain, heat, vultures, stock market speculators, bank robbers, none of them could hurt trees like this. They didn't have much to fear. Drought, maybe, or strong winds. Of course, there was fire. Fire might hurt 'em bad. But the worst would be man. Man and an axe. Men with axes and an urging to cut were the greatest enemies of these magnificent trees. Seen enough big trees chopped down in Colorado and Oregon to know that. Didn't seem right that man should be able to destroy such trees, but then lots of things didn't seem right to me.

Under the live oak canopy it was cooler, but the air was still and full of mosquitoes. One stung me on the back of the neck and I slapped at it and pushed off the tree. The ring of trees wasn't wide and beyond was a patch of turned ground. Corn grew in that black earth, and beans and some sort of taters, and what looked like pumpkins and watermelons. The woman and the two boys were at the far end of their garden, facing away from me, their hoes rising and falling in an ancient rhythm. A hound dog lay asleep at the woman's feet. Stepping out from the trees, I walked down the turned earth, taking care to step between the rows, the dirt soft and faintly damp between my toes.

Out from under the trees, I could see that there was about an hour of daylight left. A line of clouds hovered along the southern horizon, but the air didn't smell of rain. The cornstalks were a touch withered, but the beans looked good. My stomach rumbled at the thought of food.

The ground was soft and absorbed my footsteps, and I suppose they were intent on getting their hoeing done before dark. I was within five yards before the old hound lifted his head. As the hound's head came up, the woman turned.

She smiled and leaned against her hoe. I could sense the boys staring at me. I studied the woman. Her face was very round, her teeth large and white against the blackness.

"Blessed Jesus, the fever finally broke. Praise the Lord."

"How long have I been out of this world?" My voice was barely a croak.

"Since we found you. This is the third day." She shook her head and fat along her neck wobbled. "Can't say how long you were in bad shape before you stumbled across us."

"Not that long. Where are my shoes and my shirt?"

"Your shoes is under the bed, mister, but your shirt was ruint. I washed it good and cut it up into strips. Been using those strips to dress your shoulder."

Know I should have said thanks, and the words were there in my mouth. But I couldn't bring myself to give them voice.

"What about the bullet?"

"What bullet?"

"The one in my shoulder. Did you get it out?"

"Wasn't no need. Bullet went clean through you. Probably better it did. I've seen it both ways. My Uncle John, he got shot over at Tahlequah. Bullet went clean through his arm and once it healed you'd never known he'd been shot. Uncle Zeke, though, why he got hisself shot in a poker game over to the Bayou Campground. At first, it didn't seem very bad. Right in the fleshy part of his belly, hardly bothered him at all. Zeke was a big, strong man, wouldn't let nobody take the bullet out, and he did right good for a day or two. Don't know what them men was thinking. Don't guess they were. Not without a woman around to help them. Before anybody knew what was happening, infection had set in. Big Zeke lasted one day shy of two weeks after the infection commenced. Buried him one Easter Sunday morning."

A chill rippled through me. "How about me? Do I have an infection?"

"No sir," she said, "truly don't think you do. Got you all washed out good and clean. You should make it. Provided you stay away from guns, that is."

"What about my fever?"

"Shock fever, what I calls it. Most probably a doctor would have another name. But your body truly went through a horrible shock when that bullet smashed into you and tore through your hide. Then, too, you was wandering around down there by Gilman's Slough for no telling how long.

Nasty place to be. Part of what's called Big Bayou. Water's bad and they's all kinds of nasty bugs and the snakes is as thick as sticks and the air is almost blue with skeeters. No wonder you was out of your mind for a while."

My legs were starting to go and the earth was moving again, gently rising and falling like the back of one of a moving python snake. There was a ringing in my ears and my face felt warmish. I remember stumbling.

Hands grabbed my right arm. Everything was dim, not black, more like the force had gone out of the light. I felt light-headed and heavy-legged. I'd have fallen sure if that woman hadn't of been there. Gone face first into the yams. The coloreds were talking. I could hear their voices, only faintly like cotton was stuffed in my ears.

"Get ahold, Tyree. Poor man ain't well yet, just too stubborn to know better. Lots of whites is that way, men and women. That's right, son, 'tween you and me we can help him get back to the cabin. Now you boys pay no attention to what he says. Nastiest mouthed man I ever did hear. Never mind all them evil, hateful words. Always try and remember what Brother Hosea preached last time and be as much like sweet Jesus as you can. Poor man ain't in his right mind yet, that is if he has one. I'm beginning to wonder."

I heard her laugh and then that pair of little monkey boys were laughing, too. But we were walking. I could feel my body moving. Going slow, but getting somewhere. I was too weak to say anything, let alone push them away. It was all I could do to keep from falling. I purely had to hump up and take it. Take it like I had to take many a beating from my old man when I was a kid. Yes, sir, I absolutely had to take it, and that galled me right fierce.

Twenty

I WOKE UP SCREAMING and clawing the air, shattering the bad dream the way the sharp end of a stick bursts a soap bubble. Remnants of that dream dripped around the sides of my mind for a moment. Then they disappeared, leaving me sweating and shaking. Wishing I had a cigarette, I sat up on the narrow bed, catching my breath while my eyes adjusted.

Hard to say what hour of the night it was. The room was dark, but the moon was up and moonlight flowed through the open window like an alabaster river. The wind was up, too. I could hear it flicking the leaves of the live oaks and see shadows dancing on the cabin walls. Footsteps sounded against the earthen floor. Turning my head, I watched the woman come across the floor, a bulky shadow moving softly among more slender ones.

"You all right?" Her voice was thick with remembered sleep.

"I'm fine. Now go back to bed."

"I'm awake now."

"So, you'll go back to sleep. Go on, you bother me."

For all the attention she paid, I might as well have been talking to the moon. She sat at the foot of the bed and turned her face toward me. Against the blackness of her skin, her cotton gown looked like snow. I could smell her scent, sweat, honest dirt, and a faint musky smell that was troubling. I leaned back against the wall of the cabin.

"Tell the truth," she said, "I ain't been sleeping much since you arrived. Every night you talk in your sleep. Some nights most till dawn."

"What do I say?"

"Not much that makes sense, for sure. Mostly you kinda cry out like you're surprised, though sometimes when you call out a name it's about the saddest, loneliest sound I think I've ever heard."

"What names?"

"Mostly your mommy and daddy, I'd guess. Leastways they's the ones I can make out. Sometimes though you call for somebody name of Firecracker. Tonight you was calling out a new name, Johnny."

Listening to that woman tell about me talking in my sleep made me wish for a shot of whiskey. "Firecracker, that was a dog I had a long time ago, back when I was a kid."

"Where you from, mister? That is, if you don't mind my asking."

For a few seconds I didn't say anything. I was thinking it over, seeing what harm could come from telling the woman that much. Didn't seem like it would come back to haunt me. Besides, I owed her.

"Missouri," I said. "Platte County, north of Kansas City."

"Heard of Kansas City," she said. "Used to be a fellow round these parts who fancied himself a musician. Always talking about going to Chicago or Memphis or Kansas City.

Name was Arthur Bookman. Left here, must be six, seven years ago. Ever hear tell of him?"

"No," I said, "never heard the name. 'Course, I'm no musician and I haven't been home in a long time."

She nodded and her face went in and out and back into the moonlight. When the moonlight struck her exactly right, her face put me in mind of a statue I'd seen one time, although at the moment I couldn't have named the place if a loaded gun had been jammed up against my skull. Did remember that it had been a big ebony statue, full of bones and flesh, looking as though it was so full of life it was about to bust wide open.

The wind eased and the room grew quiet. I could hear her breathing mingling with the sound of a small animal rustling through the undergrowth not far from the cabin. I wondered what she was thinking. She was so big and so still you could have almost taken her for a statue. After a few minutes the quiet got on my nerves.

"Ever been to any of those places?" I asked, more to break the silence than out of actual curiosity.

She laughed a little then, softly. "Mister, in all my born days I ain't never been more than twenty miles from this place."

"Were you born here? This your home place?"

"No, the home place used to lie about a mile from here. Right where the bayou makes a big bend, but afore it joins up with Pelican Creek. My daddy's daddy built that place not long after Freedom Day, and he and my grandmother raised fourteen kids there."

She laughed then, a pleasant sound, with a natural melody woven through it. "They tell I took Momma by surprise when I was born. She'd gone down to the bayou to check on some cane poles she had set out. She was trying to catch a big old mudcat for supper. Place used to be plum full of them. Only I came on her real sudden like and she never had no time to get back to home. Poor thing hollered for her momma and lay right down there in the mud and birthed me. Daddy always said that I was sure 'nuff born down on the bayou.

"Now, my daddy was the oldest and he got the place, but it burned down after I'd got married to Luther Belmont and moved down here. My husband built this cabin, mister. Him and his brothers. They was five of them Belmont boys, all fine, good-looking strapping men, and ain't a one of them left now."

"All of them dead?"

"Deader than a hammer."

I studied her across the darkness. Moonlight streamed down her face. Never had been much of a judge of women's ages, and colored folks never show their actual years. Still, she didn't appear that old.

"How old are you?"

"Just turned thirty-four. Got married young."

"Was your husband older?"

"About a year. He got the stomach cancer. Purely ate him up alive, and me and my two babies had to sit here and watch him waste away. Couldn't have weighed no more than a hundred and thirty pounds when he died. Even got him to the doctor over to Bon Teche, but it weren't no good. My boys and I buried him under the biggest live oak out there. Wish I could have got him a stone, but there wasn't no way, no way in the world."

"All his brothers have the cancer?"

"No, none of them did. Lester, he was the youngest, died a-racing a fast car down toward Lafayette, and the oldest, that'd be Joseph, he got killed in the war. Over in France is what we was told. Army never shipped the body home. Then Murphy drowned in this very bayou, only about three miles south. Got drunk and jumped way in. Guess he never remembered until too late that he couldn't swim. The other one, Simon, well that boy never was quite right. Train smashed him to pieces one night. Sheriff said he figured Simon just stood on the rail and watched that big locomotive a-coming.

"My thought would be, God rest his soul, the man was drunk completely out of his mind. Never could handle liquor. Whiskey made him pure crazy. I married again, but Johnny Cooper was sure one bad mistake."

I nodded, but didn't say anything. That sure was a lot of death. Five boys, and all gone. Felt sorry for her. Burying your husband with your own hands had to be a right hard thing to do. I thought about Donald and Randy and the kid I'd cut down in the bank. Suddenly the dead seemed to be everywhere.

Closing my eyes, I could see the bodies piling up, stacked like cordwood. And, I thought, the dying wasn't quite finished yet. Two more to go for me, for certain. Might take me years to find them, but time was about all I had anyway.

Thinking about Johnny and Gladys made me remember something I'd been forgetting. I opened my eyes.

"Mammy?"

"Yes, sir."

"When you found me, did I have a gun? A revolver?"

"Yes, sir, you sure enough did."

"Where is it now?"

"Hid in amongst my soft clothes. Didn't want the boys to find it, you understand. Boys is naturally curious about guns and I sure didn't want no accidents. That gun still had two bullets left. I checked."

Two bullets might do it, I thought, if things went perfect. "Go get the gun," I said, "bring it to me."

She sighed and pushed up off the end of the bed. I watched her walk across the room. For a big woman she moved mighty quiet. I was tired now and wanted to lie down. But not to sleep. Not until the dreams had faded completely away. I willed myself to sit upright. Time enough for resting later. First the gun.

Seemed like she was gone a spell, but that might have been simply me feeling weak, and some afraid. I was about to call out when I saw the whiteness of her gown round the corner. For a second the moonlight caught her and she was an African painting come to life. Bones in her face stood out, her black flesh glistened, and her breasts pressed against the front of her gown, full and ripe.

Then she stepped into the shadows at the edge of the bed and stopped, holding the gun out, butt first. I took it from her and smiled at the comfort of its weight. An owl started up in the timber and I listened for a moment, remembering other times I'd heard that lonesome call late in the night. Then I nodded and said, "Thanks."

She didn't say a word. Only made a fluttering movement with her hands that made me think of butterflies. Then she turned and crossed the shadow-striped room. When she had vanished, I lay back, the revolver on my chest, its heavy metal presence comforting. For the first time in a long while I felt alive. Knowing you have to do something that needs to be done will make a man feel that way. I closed my eyes and listened to the night murmurings, thinking what I had to do, and how to do it.

Twenty-one

SUNLIGHT BASTED THE CABIN. and the live oaks, and the fields beyond. Leaning against the door frame, I peered out across the scraggly grass in the yard and through the gap in the oaks to a figure moving in a field of corn. The stalks were nearly as tall as the figure. His arms rose and fell, then rose again. I stepped out into the late afternoon.

Hot air grabbed me by the throat and my head whirled. Then I stepped into the deep shadows under the oaks and I could breathe again. For a moment, I stood in the shade, casually resting my good side against the trunk of a tree, trying to count the days since the bullet had ripped my life apart. But the days were fuzzy, as though I was looking back across them through gauze. Best I could figure was somewhere close to three weeks. The throbbing deep in the core of my shoulder let me know I still had a ways to go. I thought of Gladys and Johnny and cursed.

Sweat dampened my face and mosquitoes whined in the shade. You could smell the bayou, a ripeness so heavy it seemed almost rotten. Scents of fresh turned earth hung in the air, mingling with the sharper scent of my own sweat and the deeper, darker scent of animals who'd been there recently.

The edge of the field ran almost to the outer ring of the shade thrown by the canopy of the oaks. My shoes scuffed in the dirt and dust clouds rose. The earth was black and I bent and picked up a handful and held it to my nose. It seemed to smell of the very essence of life.

Years before, I'd shared a table with an old man from Mississippi. We were waiting for a train. The old guy was dressed in overalls and a plaid work shirt, but they were clean and his face had been razor-shaved. Over coffee, we'd got to talking and the old man had sworn that the coloreds down in his part of Mississippi ate dirt. Minerals in it, he'd said as the train chugged up. Hadn't thought of that old man since. I stuck my tongue to the dirt. It tasted of wood and fermentation and a conglomeration of flavors I couldn't name. I spit it out and walked between the corn rows toward the figure at the other end of the field.

Halfway across, I could tell it was the oldest boy and he was hoeing, chopping at the weeds, loosening the soil around the stalks. Tall for a kid, he was built lean like a sapling. But there was width to his shoulders and his arms and legs were long. Easy to see that he was going to fill in one day and make a big man. Well, his mother was a big woman, durn near as broad as she was tall and she didn't lack more than an inch of looking me in the eye.

A rain crow started cawing and the boy glanced up. When he saw me, he eased his hoe back down right in mid-chop and leaned on like it was a walking stick fancy men carry. Didn't smile or wave, but I could tell by the tilt of his head that he was watching me. I slogged on down the row, imaging that I was a big plantation owner back before the Civil War out to check on my crops and my slaves.

"Hot, ain't it?" I said when I finally reached the end of the row. Tell the truth, I was glad to stop for a minute. Wasn't that the row was all that long, more that the weakness was still on me.

The boy nodded.

I looked around for the others. All I could see was corn and dirt and a hard-boiled blue sky. Clouds were forming in the west, but they were far off and insignificant.

"You hoeing by yourself?"

"Yes, sir."

"Where's your mother and your brother?"

"Momma's gone over to see old Mrs. Oliver. She's got the rheumatism bad and sent for Momma. Momma's a kind of doctor, see. Plants and herbs and poultices. That sort of doctoring. She took Leroy with her." The boy turned his head and spat. "Leroy's still a momma's boy."

"I see. Boy, at the moment I'm disremembering your name. Want tell it to me again?"

"Tyree. Tyree Belmont."

"How old you are you, Tyree?"

"Thirteen. Almost."

"Big for your age, ain't you?"

"Reckon maybe I am." The boy struggled to keep a smile off his face.

The top of my head felt like a boiled peanut. I wiped the sweat off my face with the tail of the shirt I was wearing. The shirt was too big for me. "How come you out here hoeing by yourself?"

He shrugged and studied his bare feet. "I'm the only one there is to hoe."

"What about your step-daddy? Where's he at?"

The boy scratched idly at the dirt with the blade of his hoe. For a minute I didn't think he was going to answer. The air was hot and still, and the only sounds were the humming of unseen bees and my own faint breathing. My left shoulder throbbed some and my legs felt trembly. Then the crow cawed again, closer this time, and the boy raised his head.

"If you mean Johnny Cooper, I don't rightly know, mister. He's been gone a long time. Can barely remember what he looked like. Guess I must have been six or seven when he left. My real daddy's dead." He drug a toe through the dirt. "But I carries his name."

I let that bone lie. Another Johnny, eh? Didn't seem to be much good clinging to that name. "Where'd this Johnny go?"

The boy shrugged and gazed off in the direction of the crow. Beyond the corn was a line of poor, twisted trees flanked by weeds and brambles. Snakes live in there, I thought. My left eye started to twitch and I rubbed at it.

"Momma don't never talk none about it. I've asked my uncles and cousins, but nobody knows for sure what happened to him. Some say he run off and joined the Army. Others claim he's in the prison up to Parchman. That's in Mississippi and I've heard Johnny was born there. Some even says he's dead. Killed in a knife fight over to Baton Rouge, but I don't believe that."

"Ever ask your mother?"

"Sure, lots of times. Only that's one thing Momma won't talk about."

I didn't respond. Wasn't much I could say. Besides, I didn't feel like talking any more. My legs felt like wet hay straws and the sun seemed to be baking my brain. Maybe I shouldn't have walked so far, I told myself, at least not in the damn sun.

"You all right, mister?"

I heard the boy talking, but he sounded as if he was halfway back to the cabin. The ground seemed to move and tiny black spots no bigger than chiggers danced in front of my eyes. All I could think about was getting in the shade and sitting down.

"Not so good, boy. Reckon that bullet took more out of me than I figured." I turned to go back. Sitting under those live oaks and wishing up a breeze sounded like a plan. But the ground kept tilting and then it started spinning. I felt myself falling against the corn.

Thought I was going to taste some more of that black earth, but I only swayed. The boy got hold of me and we started hobbling down the row. I was leaning on Tyree. Those live oaks appeared to be a long way off and I wasn't for sure my legs could make it. But they held out long enough to get out of the worst of the sun and I remember easing down to the ground. Then everything went hot and black.

~ * ~

When I came around, I was sitting on the ground with my back up against a live oak. The air was still plenty hot, but the leaves knocked off most of the sun and I felt better. I looked around for the kid, but he wasn't anywhere I could see. I closed my eyes and tried to think about what I needed to do next. After a minute, I heard footsteps and opened my eyes.

The boy was walking up from the cabin, carrying a bucket and moving slow. I sat there and watched him come, thinking how pitiful I was. It was hell not being able to move like you wanted. If that had been Johnny and Gladys coming down the path, I'd have been a dead man. Right then I made up my mind not to go out again without the revolver.

For the moment, however, all I could do was sit propped up against a tree and smile at the kid standing over me. He smiled back and sat the bucket down.

"Brought you some water, mister. Here's the dipper."

I surely did despise having to drink after a colored, but sometimes a man ain't got a choice. No choice at all. The water was warm and tasted of the bucket, but I drank three full dippers before I sat the dipper back in the bucket.

"You sure was thirsty."

"Yeah, guess I was," I said. After a moment I added "Thanks."

The boy nodded and ran his toes through the dirt. He sat down against the tree beside me. He didn't say anything and I didn't either. The sun was on the slant now and the rays were coming in under the lowest branches of the oak, but the force had gone out of the light. That was the way I felt. Like the force had gone out of me.

My shoulder still hurt plenty, but I should have felt more zip. All I wanted to do was sit around and watch the sun go down. No good in that. My shoulder hurting wouldn't matter if Johnny and Gladys caught up with me. I'd have to do better than I had today. Thank God it was my left shoulder that had got shot up. Being right-handed, surely I could hold the revolver long enough to get off a couple of shots.

Thinking about shooting got me to wondering if, by chance, I had a bullet or two stashed in the pockets of my pants. I felt in my pockets, but there was only a couple of nickels, a box of matches, and a smooth rock I'd picked up in an Ozark creek so clear you could see the fine gravel lining the bottom and the trout holding still above them, flicking their tails now and then to counterbalance the current. I'd kissed a girl that day, a girl with skin like polished marble and hair the color of a brown thrush. She'd wanted me to stay and I'd often wondered what turns my life would have taken if I'd listened. But then I never had been much for listening to anybody else.

"You okay, mister?"

I jerked at the sound of the boy's voice. Getting lackadaisical on top of everything else. One way or another, I'd have to pull myself out of it.

"Yeah, I'm okay. Only daydreaming."

"I do that, too."

"Most folks do." An aching was settling in my back and I shifted position, twisting in a way that sent pain rippling all the way down my left side.

Guess something must have shown in my face 'cause the boy leaned forward and eyed me closer. "You're hurting, ain't you?"

"Some."

The boy cleared his throat. "Hope you don't mind me asking, mister, but you got shot, didn't you?"

I gave him a hard look and he lowered his head. Hell, I thought, you're a fine one, staring down a kid.

"Yeah, I got shot."

"Bet it was an accident."

"Save your money, boy. I got shot strictly on purpose."

His eyes grew big and I watched him swallow. "Must a been a real bad man to shoot you."

"I know a few of those," I said and helped myself to another drink. The water and the shade were helping considerable and the pain in my shoulder had eased off to a dull throbbing. Birds chirped above us and deeper in the stand a squirrel started squawking. A faint breeze had sprung up and its kiss was cool against my face. I closed my eyes. Peace was there amongst the trees, a greater peace than I'd known for a long time. If the boy hadn't been there watching every breath I took, maybe I'd have gone to sleep. Instead, I opened my eyes and looked off toward the cabin.

The sun was almost down and the shadows around the little cabin were deep and purple as bruises. "Learn this, boy," I said, without looking at him, "learn it early and learn it good. Life is hard and it's full of hard people. People you don't ever want to mess with." I quit talking then and scratched at a mosquito bite. From some field beyond my line of sight, cattle lowed.

"Momma says we're living in hard times."

I twisted my neck and faced the boy. His face was set and serious. The last of the daylight polished his cheeks so they glowed like rubbed bronze.

"Your momma's right about that, and hard times make hard people. Not that some people ain't born hard. Guess hard times only makes folks like that harder."

The boy nodded, keeping his eyes on me like I was some teacher or preacher, or maybe one of those Old Testament prophets who were always wandering around in the wilderness. Tell the truth, I felt a little like one sitting there beneath the massive trees.

"Bet you're a hard man when you need to be, mister," he said, without taking his eyes off my face.

I started to laugh, but instead I simply nodded and said, "Maybe I am, boy, just maybe I am a hard man when I've got cause." To myself I added, and there's at least two who are going to find us how damn hard I can be. A bead of sweat formed on my forehead and began to slide slowly down my check. It made me remember when I used to cry as a kid. I tried to remember the last time I'd cried back home.

A jaybird started up on a branch above my head and another took up the call and then another. Soon the whole grove was throbbing with the sound. Slowly, the cries died off until there was only the rising wind worrying the leaves and the faint hum of unseen insects. The boy was so quiet I thought for a second that he'd slipped away while I daydreamed, but he was still there, back against the tree, facing the cabin. From the look in his eyes, he was seeing something I couldn't see, but maybe that was natural. I sure wished I had a smoke and a shot. But then, as Mr. Davis, the school principal, had always told us in assembly, wishing got you every bit as far as hoping. A coolness was filtering through the wind now and I wondered if it would rain.

"Mister?"

The kid's voice startled me, and I took a deep breath before I answered. "Yeah."

"Can I ask you something?"

"Go ahead."

"Well, see, I was wondering..."

"Wondering what?"

"Well, I mean you don't have to tell me if you don't want to, 'cause I guess it's really none of my business, but I was wondering what your name was?"

Now, that was sure a question I hadn't expected. Suppose I could have told him any name and he'd never once known the difference. But I couldn't see how the truth would hurt. Best I'd learned, telling the truth ever once in a while never hurt anybody. "My name's Ray."

"Can I call you that?"

Right then a dog started barking. The sound seemed to come from the slough. I listened to the hound baying like he had a coon treed. Days were so quiet and lonesome like along the bayou that I'd figured this was a place not many ever came to.

"Sure, you can call me Ray. Just keep it to yourself, though. Understand?"

The boy nodded.

Now, tell me something, kid."

"What's that, mister? I mean, Ray."

"Many folks come out this way? To your place, I mean. You know, like hunters or guys fishing?"

The boy twisted his mouth up. "Some do, I reckon. Couple of the Douglas boys sure enough love to fish and there's this white gentlemen, name of Mr. Hartley, who likes to hunt in the timber down along the bayou. Squirrels is what I've seen him kill. Now and then a couple of men will pole a johnboat up near the mouth of the slough, but I don't know their names."

"Any of those men ever come up to the cabin?"

The boy scratched at his wooly head. Too bad he was a colored; otherwise, he was an okay kid.

"Mr. Hartley has come once or twice. Always gives Mamma some squirrels. Fried squirrel sure is tasty." The boy smacked his lips and I laughed without thinking.

"What about the others?"

"Oh, the Douglas boys stop by sometimes. They's some kin. Cousins, I think. Momma could tell you. Mostly they come by to visit, maybe eat a bowl of beans or a mess of greens, whatever's cooked up."

Hearing that boy talk about food got to me to thinking about eating and I realized that for the first time in a long time I was hungry. And after a meal, smoking a cigarette was mighty fine. I surely did want a smoke.

Tilting my head toward the boy, I said, "You don't happen to have a cigarette or two hid back somewhere do you, kid?"

"No, sir." He shook his head real fast. "Momma don't allow no smoking round her. That is if she can help it. Mr. Hartley, why he's a smoking fiend. Cigars and pipes. One of the Douglas boys smokes cigarettes, but Momma makes him go outside. Says she can't stand the sight of a man smoking. It's like he has a fire made by the devil inside him and the smoke's a comin' out between his lips." He shook his head again. "No sir, Mr. Ray, Momma sure don't allow no smoking. Hope you ain't accursed with the habit. Nicotine habit is evil, I hear, though not hardly as bad as the liquor one."

Well piss on that, and piss on Mammy Momma, I thought. But I kept those thoughts to myself. Boy didn't need to hear his momma put down. No boy needs that. Not even a kinky-haired Black boy. Besides, the kid had done me a good turn, and considering things honestly, I could see where I might need another good turn, or two, down the road. So, I only nodded and whistled a tune about the wreck of a train on a terrible steep curve on the downgrade. Never had learned the words straight, but it was a catchy tune.

The air was going all purple around us and shadows were blending into the dusk until you couldn't tell one from the other. A whippoorwill had started up close by. After I listened to him for a minute or two, I started pushing myself up.

Guess I could have made it, though I might have looked right awkward doing it, but the boy came over and got an arm around me and gave me something solid to lean on. In a few seconds, we were walking toward the cabin, me leaning on him a little and the whippoorwill going on and on, with the evening breeze sweet and cool against our face. Halfway to the cabin, I caught the scent of far-off rain.

Twenty-two

THE SOUND OF RAIN threaded through the darkness and I eased out of bed and padded across the floor. Hinges squeaked as I pushed the door open, but I swung it wide and stepped outside.

Earlier, the rising moon had been visible through the gaps in the tree branches. Now it was a pale halo glowing behind dark clouds. Wind whined in the live oaks and under the eaves of the cabin. Off to the west, lightning zigzagged across the blackness.

The smell of rain was stronger now, although you couldn't see it. Running through that rain smell was the sweet scent of honeysuckle. Frogs were croaking along the bayou and, out toward the trees, fireflies flickered on and off and on again. I wondered if they flickered in the rain.

Off in the distance, thunder rumbled deep and low. Lightning flashed again and the wind sent a dust devil hurling against the wall of the cabin. Standing there in the dark and the wind, I felt like I was all alone in the world, maybe the first man to ever set foot in the territory. Then, for no particular reason, I thought about Gladys and Johnny; I wondered where they were and what they were doing.

No good in going down that path. I pushed off the doorframe and strolled through the fireflies toward the live oaks. Under the trees, the darkness felt thick, heavy. I glanced up through the canopy. The sky was clouded over and the moon had disappeared. A firefly landed on my right hand and crawled up my arm, blinking as though it was signaling. I couldn't decipher the code.

A sound caught my ear and I lifted my face and looked back toward the cabin. The woman had stepped out into the yard and was slowly turning around, as though she'd lost something and was trying to find it.

For a moment I wondered what she was searching for. Then I realized she must be hunting for me. Moving carefully, I stepped deeper in the shadows until my back brushed against a thick trunk. I eased up against the tree until it seemed we were one. Standing against the tree, I wondered why I had done that. Thunder rolled in the west, rumbling on and on and on until it sounded like a slow-moving freight train. Ten yards from the cabin, the woman cocked her head and listened. She was wearing a white gown and against it her skin appeared beyond black.

She turned until she was facing in my direction. The smell of rain was thicker. I could hear the frogs again and birds stirred restlessly in the oaks. Lightning flashed, closer now. The woman started walking toward the trees. She moved slowly but surely, like a wild animal. Her feet were bare.

She crossed the open ground and stepped into the shadows. For a few seconds, she paused, then eased through the deep darkness until she was so close I could smell the natural aroma of her body. It had a peculiar scent, more like a ripe melon than anything else I could think of. Maybe all colored women smelled that way. I couldn't say. Far as I could recall, she was the first one I'd been this close to.

"You all right?' Her voice was deeper than usual.

"I'm okay."

"Not really my business, but what are you doing out here in the middle of the night with a storm blowin' in?"

I felt my shoulders shrug, then felt foolish since there was no way she could have seen the movement. I could hear thunder again, closer and sharper. "Just woke up and smelled the rain. It's been coming this way all day and I've been waiting for it. Plus, it's so hot in there I thought it might be cooler outside."

She lifted her face and sniffed as though she was smelling rain for the first time. It was truly close now. Dampness rippled through the air and I could hear the sound of falling rain down toward the bayou.

"You're gonna get wet."

"Water won't hurt."

"Guess that's true. Just didn't want you catching cold on top of everything else. Might bring the fever back."

"I've been caught out in the rain plenty of times. Never hurt me yet."

"No, a good, natural summer rain generally don't do nothing 'cept clean a body off some. My Granny Thomas used to take her bath in the rain." The woman's teeth were white in a sea of blackness.

"How's your shoulder?" Her fingers stretched out as though to touch me. I didn't move. Fingertips grazed my skin. They were smoother than I'd figured.

"Better every day."

"Good, good, that's mighty good to hear."

Rain splattered against the leaves. Then quit as suddenly as it had started.

"Tyree said you talked to him today."

"The boy and I talked a little, sure."

"He said you were a nice man."

"He's just a kid. Too young to know much."

"Still, my son's a good judge of character. He says you were nice to him and I want you to know I appreciate that. The boy gets lonesome for a man to talk to."

"It wasn't much. We only talked for a few minutes."

"He knows now you're a kind man, a good man, by his lights."

"Everybody makes mistakes."

Her scent was stronger now, as though she had inched closer in the dark. Her white gown floated like a ghost under the live oaks. I was suddenly very aware of her, aware in a way I hadn't been before. The rain started again, pecking cautiously against the leaves.

"You're right about everybody making mistakes. The Good Lord made us all in his image, but sin came forth in the Garden of Eden and since then every man and woman has been corrupted by Satan."

"Maybe so," I said, although I couldn't see what the Garden of Eden had to do with me or the boy, or, for that matter, the oncoming rain.

"And you're part of everybody, mister, so, begging your pardon, you make mistakes, too. Every soul does, white or black or red."

"What's that got to do with anything?"

"Maybe not much, but keep it in mind."

"Or what? You gonna put a spell on me, Mammy? You some sort of voodoo queen?"

"No, sir. I don't believe in voodoo or worshipping any spirits, 'cept God." She leaned closer. Her breath was warm against my face, warm and surprisingly sweet. "And if you're interested, mister, my given name is Vivian."

She paused then and I figured she was waiting for me to say something. I didn't say one word. Only listened to the rain suddenly pattering against the leaves and the warm earth.

"Now I done told you my name, you wanna tell me yours?"

"Trouble," I said.

For a moment she simply stood there. The rain was coming down harder now, sifting through the moving leaves, dampening our faces. Raindrops were cool against my bare back, and somehow that rain had the feel of a blessing.

Thought maybe I'd made her mad, but after a moment, she laughed and reached out of the darkness and pressed the palm of her left hand against my right cheek for a heartbeat or two. Her hand was smooth and cool and soft and I tried to remember the last time Gladys had touched me in that way. Thunder rumbled and she laughed again and stepped back.

"All right, Trouble. You can stay out in the rain if you want, but I'm going back to my soft dry bed. Morning seems to come powerful early these days."

I almost said goodnight, but stopped myself and after a moment she turned and walked back though the rain to the cabin, moving like some dark spirit of the rainy night. I lingered beneath those great live oaks, wishing I had a cigarette and listening to the falling rain. After a spell, the rain began to ease and I could hear the frogs down along the bayou.

Twenty-three

"HOW LONG WILL it take me to walk to town?"

The woman turned from the bed she was making. "You mean Broughton?"

"If that's the closest town," I said. "I'm looking for a real town, not a couple of vine-covered shacks at a crossroad. What I want is a place where they have stores."

"That'd be Broughton, but what you wanting to go there for?"

I fingered the bills and coins in my pocket. Had to give her an A for honesty. Far as I could tell she hadn't touched a cent. And, back when the fever was on me, she'd had plenty of chances. One of those college professors back in Missouri had told me one day that a wise man learns at least one new thing every day. Guess I'd learned that there was at least one honest colored.

"Got some things I want to buy." I could feel her eyes on me. "Like a new shirt or two."

"Huh. More like some bullets for that gun you're always fooling with."

I turned and walked over to the door and stared out across the bare packed earth that passed for a lawn. Early sunlight was still pale and you could open your mouth and taste the coolness of morning.

"Sure, I'm going to buy a box of bullets. What's wrong with that? Man never knows when he might need a loaded gun."

She snorted and popped the sheets. "A loaded gun is what almost got you killed. What you wanna go and fool with them for?"

"That's my business, Mammy."

"My name is Vivian. I done told you that."

I kept looking at the morning coming on. The boys had gone to the spring for water and the place was quiet. Too quiet to suit me. There was a deserted feeling to the cabin, as though people had lived there a long time ago and abandoned it for some unknown reason. Standing there, gazing into the trees, I felt almost alone. As though the woman and the boys were only people I'd imagined. I'd lost count of the days since I'd seen a white person. That feeling a man gets when he's held against his will was crawling over me. Jail fever, some called it.

"Like I asked already, how long to get to town?"

She didn't answer straight off and I began to wonder if she was going to ignore me. I didn't say anything, though. No colored woman was going to make me toe any kind of line, even if she had taken good care of me when I needed help. I deliberately kept my eyes on the trees.

Voices drifted across the morning, faint and distorted. They sounded as if they were coming from the bayou. Fishermen, I figured. I hoped to be long gone before they got here. More reason for me to be moving.

"Depends, I guess."

I heard the mattress sigh, turned, and looked across the cabin. The woman was sitting down on her bed. She had a sad expression on her face, as though life had disappointed her again. Well, I had news for her—life was nothing but one day of disappointments after another.

"Depends on what?"

"Whether you want to go by the road or cut across."

"Guess cutting across is quicker?"

She nodded. "Save you a good three, four hours. Have to backtrack across some fields to get to the road and it does some powerful winding once you reach it. Walking's easier, of course, but it does take longer."

"I'll cut across. Can you draw me a map?"

She shook her head and sighed. Then she pushed her body off the bed, grunting a little. "Map would be way too hard to draw. More twists than a snake. Even if I drew you one, you'd still get lost. No, somebody will have to go with you and I can't go off and leave Leroy. He's way too young for that. Guess Tyree will have to go with you. He's been four, five times. Knows the way pretty good by now."

"Just draw me a map, Mammy. I surely don't want no picaninny with me when I go to town."

She gave me a hard look and bit her fat lower lip. Then she ambled over and uncovered a plate of cold cornbread, picked up a wedge, and bit off a chunk. "You said your name was Trouble and I'm beginning to think you wasn't joking, 'cause you sure is a lot of trouble. Plum ungrateful, to boot. I know you don't like me, but you don't have to rub my face in it. I got feelings, too, you know. Even if I am just a nigger to you."

After she made that speech, I did feel bad for a few seconds. After all, she had saved my life. But then I told myself she was nothing special to me and I made my mind hard.

I didn't say anything and she didn't either. Instead, we stared at each other. I'd not noticed before how big her eyes were. Big and dark and sad. Like they'd seen some real hard times. I couldn't help but feel sorry for the woman.

"All right, all right, Mammy, I'm sorry I hurt your feelings. Now, tell me how to get to this Broughton. I need to get moving before the day heats up."

"My name is Vivian."

I closed my eyes, took a deep breath, and promised myself that before I left I'd give her a beating she wouldn't never forget. It took me two tries and I had to swallow hard, but I finally spit it out: "Vivian."

"Thank you. Person likes to hear their own name once in a while and you've got a real pleasant voice, when you want to use it."

Anger was rising in me, but I choked it back. First the bullets. Then the payback.

"Now, like I was saying, mister." She stopped talking and smiled. "Sure wish you'd tell me your given name. Don't seem natural calling you Mister, or Trouble."

"Don't worry about my name. Tell me how to get to Broughton."

"Like I done told you, somebody's going to have to show you. Easy way would be to cut across Joe Curry's field and hit the highway. You could catch it at the crossroads. Big old catalpa tree grows right there. Biggest anybody around here ever heard tell of. Couldn't miss it if you wanted to. But then you have to go clear up to Lee's Ford and cross on the concrete bridge. That's what I mean by wandering. No shade to speak of most of the way and you'd have to rest considerable. Shape you're in, don't believe you could walk to Broughton that way in a day. Better way is to cut along the bayou and find you a boat to ferry you across. It's harder walking, but heaps faster. You sure you up for some tough walking?"

She was staring at me like she doubted I could walk across the cabin. I stared right back at her and nodded. "I can make it," I said. Sometimes she made me mad as hell, but still I recognized she'd taken good care of me; I owed her. She was nice, too. Nice in a sweet, warm comforting way. She was sure no beauty queen and way too heavy. But she had a comforting way about her and, much as it pained me to admit it, her lips did look mighty soft and inviting. I wondered if the fever had affected my brain.

"Boys will be back soon and Tyree can go with you. Once you get to town, he can hang back so you won't be embarrassed. Now, we don't want a fine white man like you to be seen with no black boy, now do we, Trouble?"

"Least you got that right, Vivian," I said. Her name was a sharp stone in my mouth.

She rubbed her hands together and the fleshy part of her arm above the elbow jiggled. Then she smiled. On the witness stand, I'd have to admit she had a nice smile. But I wasn't on no witness stand, and didn't aim to ever be on one. I'd settle my affairs in my own way.

"'Spect I'd better fix you all up a poke of food to take along. We got cornbread from supper and they's still a little chicken left. I'll wrap it all up in a towel for you to carry along. Even cutting across, you're looking at a half-day's walk, and you ain't a man what's got his true strength back yet." She took a step toward me and gazed up at my face. "Sure you won't wait, Trouble? Maybe another day or two, so you can get more strength back?"

I didn't say anything, but she read the answer in my face.

"All right, then. I'll get started on that poke, and I'm gonna make you and Tyree a good strong cup of coffee to drink before you strike out."

She kept looking at me like she expected me to say something. Thank her, I suppose. That'd be the day. I'd said her name and that was enough for this white man to swallow.

She reached out and brushed her fingertips down my forearm. All touching made me nervous, and her touching me was twice as bad. I could feel my nerves singing and the heat was rising in my face. She turned without speaking and walked toward the rear of the cabin. I went and put on my shirt and drug my gun out from under the mattress. After making sure the safety was on, I jammed it down in the right front pocket of my pants.

I glanced down. If you looked close, you could see a bulge sure enough, but you couldn't tell exactly what was making it. A good coffee smell began to fill the room and I knew I'd drink a cup before I left. Have to give fat Vivian credit—the woman sure enough had some good qualities. I sat down on the bed and watched her wrap the leftover chicken in a clean dishtowel. I closed my eyes and thought about Gladys and Johnny. Wouldn't those two be surprised to see me? My lips curled into a smile of their own accord and I opened my eyes, pushed up and started walking across the room.

Twenty-four

For the first hour the walking was easy. We followed a curving path worn smooth as it meandered through open meadows and along sagging fence lines, slipping now and then between willows and poplars and gum trees as big around as the belly of a horse. The morning was pleasantly cool and my muscles warmed up gradually. A fine sheet of sweat dampened Tyree's forehead. All the time we could hear the slough, gurgling and sloshing off to our north, but we did not go there.

The land began to gently roll and the grasses grew taller and the path narrowed as though many of those who had come before had abandoned the way. Tiredness had begun to work its way up my legs and I could tell that Vivian was right—I still didn't have all my strength back. Didn't say anything though, even when I noticed the kid looking back.

The sun was almost overhead when we came down a slope and out into a weedy patch dotted with cedars and sassafras. White rocks jutted up through the ground and I hollered at the kid and we sat down on a flat one. I split up the chicken and the cornbread and we drank lukewarm water out of a Mason jar the boy had been carrying. The chicken was greasy, but I was glad to rest my legs. My shoulder had started to throb and I wondered if I'd ever be whole again. Then I thought about what I'd like to do to Gladys and Johnny. Guess I thought on that a little long 'cause the boy cleared his throat and said, "You all right, Mister Ray?"

"Sure," I said, "Just getting old, kid."

He laughed a little at that and then said, "You ain't old, Mister Ray."

"Maybe not, but I've had a hard life."

He nodded like I'd said something worth remembering.

I took a sip of water, wishing it was whiskey. "How much farther, Tyree?"

The boy lifted a hand and pointed to the northeast. "Not so very far as the crow flies, Mr. Ray, but there ain't no straight way to get there." He sighed and turned back to face me. "Two ways to go. One is the long way around, go clear up to Broussard's Bend and cross the bayou on the bridge. The walking ain't too bad, but it takes considerable time."

I wiped sweat off my forehead. Louisiana sunlight showed no pity or mercy. "What's the other way?"

Tyree grinned. "The other way is to walk down along the side of the bayou and see if we can find us a johnboat or a pirogue to get across in. Sometimes there's an old man who will take you across for two bits. But he's a right nasty man."

"Well, so am I. Let's get going."

Tyree grinned bigger, stood, and started walking down the slope. I pushed myself off the rock and followed him. As the grasses grew taller, trees leaned across the narrow path and their limbs twisted into each other. Insects whined and strange sounding birds cried out. I felt like I was on one of those jungle safaris you sometimes see written up in newspapers.

In ten minutes, the ground had gone mucky and the shade was so deep it looked like twilight. You couldn't see the water yet, but you could sure enough smell it. The odor was more like rotting vegetation than anything else and there was something truly old in that bayou smell. As old as time itself, I thought, wondering how many millions of years the bayou had been there.

"This bayou got a name?"

Tyree paused, one foot on a fallen tree trunk. "Don't know its rightful name. Folks around here just call it the bayou, or the swamp."

A mosquito stung me on my neck and I slapped at it. My hand came back with blood on it. Maybe it was my imagination, but it was like you could smell disease growing. I'd been in unhealthy places before, but this had to be the worst. Through gnarled trees I could see water, so dark it was almost black. As I watched, a V spread out from the bank. Seconds later I could see a snake, black as licorice and thick as my arm, swimming for the far bank.

"Time to move on, boy," I said and started walking. Mud was already settling around my shoes and they came free with a plop. Swarms of mosquitoes hovered in front of us and bugs crawled on my arms. Spider webs hung down from tree branches and you could hear rustlings in the underbrush. Sweat coated my skin and had soaked through my shirt and trousers. I hoped we'd find a boat or the old man real soon. The kid kept plodding ahead. I told myself if he could do it, then so could I. After a while it occurred to me that about the only thing this pestilent place might be good for was getting rid of bodies. Despite the sweat and mosquitoes, I found myself grinning.

~ * ~

Twenty minutes later, we pushed our way out of a mangrove swamp and stepped into blinding sunlight. The heat was so intense it felt like we'd stumbled into the belly of a blast furnace by mistake. My head swam and sweat stung both eyes. I swiped at the sweat, coating my forehead with the back of a hand, and blinked at the sweat in my eyes. The boy said something, but there was a ringing in my ears and I had a high, hollow feeling inside my skull.

When the dizziness passed, I could see the boy about ten yards in front of me, pointing toward the water and saying something. I still wasn't hearing good and took a cautious step closer.

"What is it, kid?"

"The boat, Mr. Ray, there's the boat we can use to get across."

I could see it now, a long, low-slung vessel carved out of dark wood. In one of my schoolbooks there had been a drawing of a boat a lot like it. Took me a minute to recall the name. Dugout.

"Where's the old man you were telling me about?"

"Probably back in the shade somewhere." The kid's black face shone with sweat. He wiped at it with an old rag he carried jammed in his pants. "Sure is a hot one today, ain't it?"

"Way too damn hot to stand out here in the sunlight jabbering like a couple of crows. Let's get down there and see if we can roust that old man out. Besides, the boat is already sitting in the shade. Bound to be some cooler there."

The boy nodded and we trudged down the hill. More than ever, I felt like Cortez, or one of those old Spanish explorers Miss Grisholm used to talk about back in school. As I remembered the stories, most of them came to a bad end. Wished I'd paid better attention.

Out of the direct sunlight, the air was still smoldering, but the force of the sun was diluted and a man felt like he might survive. The boat was tied up to a willow and floated smooth and free. Neither the boy nor I could see or hear the old man, but my gut kept telling me he was out there, hidden behind a tree or in a patch of horseweeds, watching us. I hollered a couple of times, but he didn't answer. I nodded at the boat and the boy stepped over the side and sat down on a plank stretched across the boat. Holding on to the willow with one hand, I started to climb in after him. The ground had gone to muck around the boat and for a second my shoes stuck and I thought they were coming off, but I gave my legs a good tug, one at a time, and my shoes came free and I swung my legs over the side of the dugout,

With both of us in it, the boat rode lower in the water. Too low to suit me, but I'm more a car guy. We sat there for what seemed like an hour, rocking gently on the brown water, slapping at black flies and mosquitoes, and looking around for the old man. I was tempted to untie and push off, but I didn't know the land here, or the people, and I sure as hell didn't know this bayou.

It looked like an easy trip across, but appearances can be deceiving and I'd heard tales about alligators and I knew for personal certain that snakes swam in these waters. We sat quietly on the plank, listening to the soft sloshing of the water and the whine of insects and the harsh call of a bird that sounded like a cross between a crow and a jay. After a few minutes, the boy started whistling a tune. He whistled soft, a mournful tune if I ever heard one. Made me about half want to shoot myself. Then a woodpecker started hammering like he'd gone crazy. The entire bank was full of trees and it took me some time to track him down. He was beating the bark of a huge old sycamore that was deader than a hammer. Just as I was fixing to point him out to the boy, I heard a branch crackle and turned in time to see a shadow move. I put a hand over Tyree's mouth and he looked up at me like I'd gone crazy.

The shadow moved again and then it stepped out of the trees and I could see it was an old man—undoubtedly the skinniest man I had ever seen. He was tall enough and dressed in overalls, gum boots, and a greasy long-billed cap that covered his head and slanted down so it hid the top part of his face. The bottom part was mostly bone and lips. Ten feet away, the lips came apart, revealing large yellow teeth. One front tooth was missing, or rather broke off.

"That's my boat you're sitting in."

I took my hand off Tyree's mouth. "That's all we're doing. Just sitting. Ain't no harm in sitting, is there?"

"Guess that all depends," the old man said. He pushed the cap off his forehead and you could see how pale his skin was underneath. His arms were bare below the elbow and deeply tanned. Muscles in his arms were visible and the veins were thick, like overfed worms. I eased one hand down in the pocket where the revolver was. "What you boys a figuring to do?"

The boat was shaking a little and I glanced over at Tyree. One leg was going up and down like a pneumatic drill. Trying to act natural, I reached over and put a hand on top of his knee.

"All we want to do is get a ride across. Think maybe you could take us?"

"Mayhaps, I could, but let's talk money first."

"Sounds right," I said. "How much?"

The man ran a hand along his jaw. I could sense his eyes on me, sizing me up, trying to judge how much he could get out of me. I sat and waited. Waiting never hurt a man when he was talking price."

"Four bits for you, and two for the boy there."

"Fair enough."

"Let's see your money."

I took my hand off Tyree's leg and dug two quarters, two dimes, and a nickel out of my pocket. I stretched out my arm and dropped the coins in his hand. Fingers closed like a claw.

He didn't say anymore, only gave me a look I couldn't decipher and untied the rope. Then, as smooth as though he was walking up the steps to his own house, the old man stepped in the boat, bent, and tugged out a long pole that had been angled across the boat bottom. He jammed the pole into the water like a knife sliding into soft butter. The water barely swirled. He pushed off against the bottom and we floated away from the bank. The bayou must have been fairly shallow all the way across because the old man kept staring at me and pushing with his pole. Only now and then, he'd turn his head and spit a stream of tobacco juice.

I kept one eye on the old man and the other on the water, searching for gators or snakes. I could feel the boy beside me. He was trying to act tough, but his body was trembling. Halfway across, I stretched out an arm and wrapped it around his shoulders.

The old man grunted and maybe he said something, but I couldn't swear it. Now I'd never been no daddy and had no plans to be, but somehow right in the middle of all that dark water I felt the way I imagined one would feel, at least for a few minutes.

Twenty-five

ONCE YOU CLIMBED OUT of the bottom, you walked along a sunken road that ran between two lines of overarching trees and the road was sand and the going was soft and walking down it made your legs ache. After a mile or two, the feeling that you might have to walk damn near to forever started to grow on you. Then you came around the bend and there was the town, sprawled along both sides of the road, looking like a painting by a well-meaning amateur.

Not that Broughton was much of a town. Nothing more than one main street of hard packed sand with four or five side streets meandering off, apparently at random. Low slung, wooden store buildings lined the main street, but the bank on one corner was brick. At the far end of the street were two churches. Both were made of wood and painted white and both had steeples. They stood on opposite sides of the street. Beyond the churches were patches of grass and then the trees started up again.

The boy and I walked down the road together, but before we reached the first store I tapped him on the shoulder and nodded at the side of the building. A narrow patch of blue shade ran the length of the structure. It felt good to get out of the sun. High noon had come and gone and the light was coming in on the slant now, but it still had plenty of force.

I bent down and looked the kid in the eyes. Now that I was here, I didn't need him, and I sure couldn't have him tagging along. Problem was I didn't know what to do with him. Didn't seem right to just leave him.

"Tyree, I've got some business to tend to and I can't take you along. Understand?"

"Sure, Mr. Ray."

"Well good," I said, and feeling better, plus a little generous, I reached in my pocket and pulled out two quarters. "Hold out your hand," I said, and dropped them in his open palm. "You can buy yourself some crackers and a soda pop with those, I guess." I looked around for a place that would be safe for a kid to wait. I'd heard stories about what some peckerwoods would do to a boy like Tyree. Nothing struck me as right until I thought of the churches.

"There's two churches up at the end of the street. They'll be a graveyard behind one of them, sure. Know where I'm talking about?"

"Sure, I've been there before."

"You have?"

He nodded. "With Mama."

My shoulder was acting up and I rubbed it. It was noticeably cooler in the shade, but it still felt like ninety degrees. The air had gone dead still and the afternoon lay heavy on the sleepy town.

"Then you know where to go. I'll see you there later. Okay?"

"Mr. Ray?"

"What?"

"'Stead of the graveyard, can I go to my uncle's house?"

"Your uncle lives in Broughton?" I could see that there was a lot I didn't know and I wasn't crazy about finding it out in pieces.

"Sure enough. My uncle Tobias, he lives over there." The boy pointed at one of the side streets. "Uncle Tobias is my mother's older brother. We come to his place for special days, like Thanksgiving and Christmas."

The boy was grinning at the thought of seeing his folks. Couldn't blame him for that. Tell the truth, I'd have been right glad to see a few of my kin. Didn't have the heart to pop his red balloon, but there were questions.

"What if your uncle ain't home?"

"Oh, Uncle Tobias, he's always at home. See, he ain't got but one good leg and don't go around much, save to his jobs and to church on Sundays. Then he rides in Artis Webster's wagon. And this ain't Sunday."

That stopped me for a minute. I hadn't even considered the day. What a rube. I could just as easy have shown up on a Sunday, and then where would I be. A church-going man wasn't what I was cut out for. Although, after what I'd been through lately, there was one passage out of the Bible that made sense to me, and that was an eye for an eye. Straight out of the Old Testament. I could hear those old Missouri preachers giving it the power and the glory as they read the Word of God from the pulpit on Sunday mornings.

Once I caught up to a certain pair of sinners, I planned to quote it to them as they stared down the barrel of my pistol. Maybe they'd get religion before I pulled the trigger. Wasn't sure if you could get to heaven without being baptized, but I had no intentions of sprinkling their heads with holy water. Then again, I just might immerse them in the bayou once they'd breathed their last. Thinking about that made me grin.

Out on the sand road, a wagon rolled by, two flop-eared mules pulling it. A man with hair sticking up like porcupine quills held the reins. The mules and the man had their heads down and they never glanced right or left. Three or four feeds sacks were stacked up in the wagon box. The mules plodded along in the middle of the road, ears twitching now and then as they flicked away flies. Their hooves made soft thudding sounds as they struck the road bed.

"All right then, kid, go to your uncle's. I'll find you when I'm finished." A fly landed on my nose and I jerked my head. "How will I know the right house?"

Tyree turned and pointed toward the north side of the main street. "See that second street down there, the one on the far side of that building with the flag sticking out of it?"

"Yeah."

"Well, turn down that street and my uncle's house is the third one on the right. Got a blue door. Got a picket fence in front of it, but the gate ain't never locked."

"Okay," I said, "now run along and I'll see you in a bit."

The boy stuck out his hand. The two quarters shone against his palm. "Here's your money back. My uncle Tobias, he'll feed me good. Always some kind of pie cooked up in that house."

"Keep it, kid, and get moving. Best for us not to be seen together by too many people."

For a moment he simply looked up at me. Then he grinned, turned, and trotted across the street at an angle. I stood in the shadows and watched him until he turned the corner. When he had disappeared, I wiped my face, tucked my shirttail in and stepped out into the empty street.

After a block there was a wooden sidewalk in front of the stores and most of the stores had awnings. A few of the stores had benches in front of them, but they were all empty. Too hot, I figured, although it had to be cooler sitting than walking.

The first store was boarded up and the second one looked like a notions store for women. But there was a hardware store on the corner and I turned and walked in. After the sunlight it was like night inside and I paused to let my eyes adjust. I could hear people talking, but the voices sounded like they were coming from the back of the store. I closed my eyes and when I opened them, I could see a long row of tools hanging by hooks hammered into the wall. Hoes and sickles and axes, that sort of thing. There were racks of overalls and plaid shirts and jackets a farmer might wear. A barrel of nails stood next to a pyramid of feed sacks. The place smelled of dust, dirt, cattle feed, and linseed oil. I looked around for the guns.

They were in glass cases jammed against the wall behind the counter. A bald man sat on a stool in front of them. He was chewing on a pencil and staring at me. I nodded.

"Help you?"

"Got any pistol ammunition?"

"Believe we can help you." He jerked his head. "Come on over."

Floorboards squeaked beneath my shoes. The wood was dark with age, dirt, and oil. I marched on up to the counter. Baldy was studying my face. Strangers must not pass through Broughton much. He would remember me. So be it; I aimed to be long gone before anybody even thought of looking.

I pulled the pistol out of my pocket and laid it on the counter. "For this one. A full box."

The man eyeballed the pistol. Then he turned and ran his hand along a row of boxes on a low shelf, pulled one out and sat it on the counter beside the pistol. "Two-fifty."

I pulled my billfold out of a back pocket and dug out three ones. He rang up the sale and slid a fifty-cent piece across the counter. I picked up the coin and the box of bullets and the pistol and started to go. Then I remembered.

I pulled my wallet back out and fingered the picture out. The water stain was faint. I placed it on the counter. One corner was bent and I smoothed it out. The man lowered his head. A tiny red mark marked the very top of his bald pate. It was shaped like a crescent moon.

"Pretty girl," he said.

"Yeah," I said, "have you seen her?"

The man picked up the picture. He picked it up carefully, by one corner, the way a woman might pluck a flower from her garden, turning it to catch the light.

"Well?"

He looked me in the face and shrugged. I stuck out my hand and he laid the photo in my palm as though it was a communion wafer.

"Can't say for sure, but maybe." He rubbed his hand back and forth across the top of his head, as though he was polishing his skull. "Now, the light wasn't good, and I'd had a beer or two, but yeah, maybe."

Before I slipped it back in the wallet, I glanced at the photo. Why I bothered I don't know. Her face was the one I'd never forget. Not if I lived to be a hundred.

"Where'd you see her?"

Baldy shrugged again. "Beer joint about a mile out of town. Name's Jacques' Place. It's on the old Clintonville Road."

"Was she with anybody?"

"Like who?"

"Say a man about my age, a little shorter and thinner. With a scar on his jaw. Right here." I ran a forefinger along the tip of my jaw. "Looks like a fishing hook."

"Don't know if she was with anyone particular. See, it was a Friday night a couple of weeks ago and the place was crowded. Lots of guys had got paid, I guess. Anyway, the place was packed. 'Course, it's a cracker box to start with. Everybody was moving around, talking and carrying on, real loud like. Plus, there was this band playing. Bunch of Cajuns making a racket. So loud you could hardly hear the guy next to you talking. So no, mister, I couldn't say she was with anyone or not. Really, can't swear it was even her. Still, she did favor your photo."

"Was she dancing?"

"Let me think." The man rolled his eyes up like he was trying to see inside his brain. My hands had started trembling. I jammed them down in my pockets.

"Yeah, maybe she was dancing. Yeah, sure she was. I remember now. At least once I saw her dancing. The light, see. I remember the way her hair caught the light. Looked like gold melting. She's a blonde, ain't that right?"

I nodded.

"Sure hope you find her, mister. She your wife?"

"Something like that," I said as I turned and headed toward the street.

"Come back anytime," the man called after me.

I lifted a hand and kept walking.

Twenty-six

THE MAN BEHIND the bar handed me back the photograph. The bent corner was torn now and grease marks smudged the bottom. Dozens of strange men had handled the photo and it had taken on a grimy, used feel, and in my mind that feeling was settling on Gladys. But that was foolishness. She wasn't here and maybe never had been. The joint was made out of concrete blocks and tin, and the heat was intense. My shirt was soaked with sweat, and the stench of unwashed bodies was stronger than the smell of stale beer and Brilliantine. The band was lousy, and loud. I leaned over the counter, shouted "Thanks," and started walking for the door.

Hard dark had settled in, and I stood outside the door for a minute, peering out into the blackness, wondering what time it was. The moon was up, but clouds dotted the sky and it was difficult to get a reading. The night had that after midnight feeling, but that may have been the effect of too much beer. My brain throbbed. I should have eaten more peanuts.

In the broken moonlight, the gravel drive could almost have passed for alabaster, and I walked down it toward the road. Gravel crunched beneath my feet and birds were restless in the trees. The smell of pines was sharp. At the edge of the highway, I bent left and headed for town. My head was starting to clear and my legs moved smoothly and a feeling that I could walk all the way to the Gulf of Mexico surged through me. But that was only beer foolishness, and I wiped the sweat off my face and kept walking.

The pistol and the box of bullets were heavy in my pockets, but they were a comforting weight. Before I started hitting the juke joints and honky-tonks, I'd stopped in a patch of moonlight and loaded the cylinder. Knowing he can defend himself gives a man confidence, and I marched along with my head up and my chin out.

Twenty-seven

WHATEVER LIFE HAD BEEN in the town earlier had died. The slap of my shoes against the pavement echoed off the buildings. Here and there light still burned behind curtains, but most of the buildings were dark. I walked to the building with the flagpole without seeing anything more vicious than a stub-tailed tomcat and turned down the side street that was scarcely more than a dirt road with a gravel sprinkled on top like confetti. The moon had popped out through a break in the clouds and I found the picket fence easy enough.

The back of my neck went cool as I stepped into the yard. I took a good grip on the butt of the pistol. For as far as I could see, all the houses were dark, although I could faintly hear someone strumming a guitar, accompanied by low throaty voices. In the moonlight, the house in front of me leaned toward its neighbor on the right. A big old mulberry tree grew close against the porch. Under its branches the ground was black.

Halfway across the yard, a voice from the porch called out.

"Who goes there?"

I wasn't expecting to be called out and I jerked like I'd been stung. Gripping the butt harder, I eased it up an inch and stopped walking. My heart was hammering against my chest.

"I'm looking for Tyree."

"You the man my sister wrote me about?"

"That'd be me."

"What's your name, mister?"

"My name is Ray," I said.

"Guess you're all right then," the voice from the shadows said. Floorboards squeaked and a man stepped out of the shadows. The fella stood at the edge of the porch, a single barrel shotgun cradled in his arms. I was glad to see the barrel pointed away from me. "Ray is what Tyree called you. Boy seems to like you, and I trust his judgment about people. Smarter than his mama in that way."

I didn't quite know how to take that last remark, so I ignored it. My heart was starting to slow, but I'd started sweating. Never had trusted a colored yet, and I didn't aim to start with one holding a shotgun on me. Well, I guess the kid was okay, but that was it as far as I was concerned. Kids ain't quite coloreds anyway, least not till they growed up. I wondered what sorta man Tyree would make. Then I thought about the kind of man I'd turned out to be.

"You must be his uncle Tobias," I said.

The man nodded. He had a long face, like a horse's, but his bones were chiseled sharp. Standing in the quirky light, he put me in mind of an Indian chief I'd seen once out in Tahlequah, Oklahoma. I tried to remember that old boy's tribe. Blackfoot maybe, or Osage.

"Tobias Miller, that's me. Been that for forty-three years." The man leaned the shotgun against a porch pillar and I took my hand off the pistol. I hoped he wasn't aiming to try and shake hands; I couldn't abide shaking hands with a colored.

"Getting powerful late," he said. "We about give you up coming. Rest of 'em done gone to bed."

"Tyree, too?"

"Oh my, yes, that boy was plum wore to the bone. Ate him a big old pork chop and a sweet potato, then went to sleep sitting up. I laid him down on the shucky bed. You must have walked that boy powerful hard, mister."

"I was aiming to start back tonight," I said.

"Well, you can forget that. That boy needs his sleep. Besides, there's not a safe place to sleep between here and Vivian's. If the snakes or the gators don't get you, then the riffraff will."

"Riffraff?"

"Half the people in this county is nothing more than hoodlums. Some runs shine, and others earn their living robbing and stealing from decent folks. Recent days, some of them gangsters from up north has come into the territory and started robbing banks. They done hit the bank over to McAllister and I heard tell they robbed the one at Lindstrom's Crossing." He paused and eyed me from the porch. "Where you from, mister, if you don't mind my asking?"

"Come from a lot of places," I said, "but started out back in Missouri, close on the Kansas border."

"Tyree said when they found you that you'd been shot and was out of your mind with the fever."

"The boy told the truth."

"Mind telling me how you got shot?"

"That's a personal matter," I said.

"Since you living with my sister and traipsing all over Louisiana with my nephew, I guess I got a right to know," he said.

There was a harder edge to his voice, like he'd sharpened it on a whetstone. I spoke against that edge. "Ain't nothing to get too excited about. Got shot over a woman. Don't reckon I'm the first."

"'Spect not," he said. His head turned slowly, surveying the street. "Sheriff Boudreaux, he rolls up and down the street now and then. Also, some of them bootleggers over to McKissock travel the roads at night. Might strike them as strange, a white man standing in a colored's yard. You wanna come in? We ain't no Monteleone Hotel, but I could give you a place to lay your head, and a pillow and a blanket to go with it."

"Wouldn't want to disturb the others," I said. "You got anyplace else? Barn or shed, maybe?"

"Nothing, only the old pony shed. Man I bought this place from, name was Lothair Groshen, was crazy for horses. After he got old he couldn't hardly take care of a regular horse or mule, so he took up raising ponies. Shetlands, he called them. Got 'em from up in Kentucky. Claimed they used them in the coal mines to pull out the coal. You reckon that's so, mister?"

"Couldn't say." I rubbed at the tiredness in my eyes. "What time is it, anyway?"

"Last I checked the mantle clock, it had gone quarter past midnight, and that was a good twenty minutes ago."

"No wonder my eyes are heavy. Reckon I might take you up on that pony barn, and a blanket, if you got extra."

"Don't want no pillow?"

"Nope. Got used to sleeping without one."

"Where in world you do that?"

"Texas," I said, which was the truth. Part of it, anyway. Rest of the story was that I'd learned to sleep on nothing more than a few wooden slats hammered together. Done that in the Brownsville jailhouse. Thirty days for breaking and entering. Sheriff out there caught me before I'd found anything worth taking, or I'd got a lot more time than that. Can't stand a pillow now. Too soft.

"Do tell," the colored said. "Never heard of such, but this world is a strange and wonderful creation, I reckon. Now, you hold on and I'll grab that blanket, then walk you down there. There are a couple of sinkholes in the yard, and if you don't know where to step you might crill your ankle."

I nodded, and he picked up the shotgun, turned, and walked across the porch, dragging one leg. I heard the screen door screech open and then the night fell quiet. After a bit, I could hear tree frogs and an owl off in the woods beyond the house. Then I heard a funny sound. Took me a minute to figure out it was somebody snoring. Somehow the snoring sounded like a woman's snoring to me, although I don't know if you can truly tell. Gladys never snored, only made ladylike breathing sounds, little puffs. Far as I knew, I'd never heard Vivian make any noise in the night, only her regular deep breathing, which, for a reason I couldn't name, sometimes sounded to me like it was the very earth itself breathing.

The screen door screeched again and then the man hobbled down the steps, a lantern dangling from one hand. Yellowish light fell around him like broken glass. He motioned with his head, and we walked around the house and across the grass. He was a tall man, a good five or six inches taller than me, but streamlined. He favored one leg some, but moved better than I'd expected after hearing the boy talk about him. After a few strides, I could see the bulk of the pony barn at the edge of the trees. Neither of us spoke as we eased down a gentle slope.

Two men out for a late-night stroll. I wondered what the sheriff would think if he happened to roll by. No doubt he'd seen stranger sights. Before we got to the barn, really more of a lean-to, I could smell old hay and the faint scent of horses, plus a dozen other aromas I couldn't name. Off to the north, a dog barked in the night, and a puff of a breeze blew cool across my face.

"Well, mister, here we are."

I peered through a deep darkness. Out of that darkness a silhouette emerged, shape shifting in the moving shadows. One moment it looked like a decapitated barn, the next like a mountain being born.

"Sorta open, isn't it?"

"Like I told you, it was a kind of stable for horses. Always figured the old man aimed to finish it, but got sick afore he got the job done. Bought it as is, see. Bought everything, even the six ponies he had left. 'Course, there's only one left now."

"You mean there's a horse in there?"

The man laughed a little then, and I figured he was laughing at me. If it hadn't been for the kid, I might have pistol whipped that big colored, or had me a go at it anyway.

"Ain't but one little pony, and Jo-Jo won't bother you at all. Oh, he might sniff around some on you. Smellingest pony I ever did run across. Like a dog that way. 'Course, you don't have to sleep here if you don't want to. Town ain't got no hotel, that's true enough, but the cemeteries is both kept mowed pretty good and I don't 'spect the dead will bother you none." He laughed again. Must have thought he was a comedian.

"I'll sleep here. Slept in lots worse places than this. Only thought from the way you described it that it was more like a barn, with doors that latched and all."

"No, no doors, but there's plenty of good clean straw. Pitchforked some in there yesterday. Stay down on this end and you'll be fine. Jo-Jo's tied up at the other end. Rope's too short to let him bother you any down here."

"I'll be fine," I said.

"Why sure you will," he said. "Here's you a blanket. It'll cool off some before daylight, so a light cover might feel good. Lest ways, you could spread it out and lay down on top of it. Straw will poke and scratch a fellow some till he gets it broke in."

"Thanks," I said. "I'll be up to the house early to get the boy. We got a long walk back and I'd like to get some of it behind me before the heat builds."

In the lantern light I could see his head nod. "Understand that."

He held the lantern high and I could see the open shed and the straw covering the ground. "Guess I'll wish you good night then."

"Night," I said. Then I said, "Thanks." Had to choke a big knot down to get that word out, but I got it out. I was still afraid he'd want to shake hands. Some coloreds was getting that way. And uppity coloreds were nothing but trouble, Johnny claimed, and I suppose, in a way, he was right about that.

But Tyree's uncle only nodded, turned, and started back to the house. I watched the lantern bob in the darkness until it was no more than a speck of light. When even that disappeared, I eased my way toward the shed, feeling ahead with one hand so I wouldn't bump into it.

When I was a kid, I'd slept in a barn a few times and the straw in Louisiana felt exactly like the straw in Missouri. I lay on my back and stared up through the cracks in the roof of the shed. Stars were out, surrounding a curling slice of moon, and I could hear creatures rustling around in the timber. The breeze had grown stronger and there was a strain of coolness running through it.

For a long time, I thought about Gladys and Johnny, wondering where they were tonight, and if they were asleep, or making love, or thinking about what they would do to me when they finally found me. That's what they should have been doing—thinking about how they were going to finish me off, because I sure as hell knew what I aimed to do when I finally caught up with them.

Thinking about them made my head ache, so I turned over and listened to the pony breathing and snorting, stamping his feet now and then. After a while, I got to thinking about Tyree and his uncle. For coloreds, I guessed they was all right.

I could feel my mind smoothing out and I tried to say a short prayer. You never knew. Only, for some strange reason, I got to thinking about Vivian, and, in a way, I sort of missed hearing her deep breathing in the night. Missed it the way you miss the cast that protected your broken arm after the bone heals and the cast is removed. Suppose, in a peculiar sort of way, your mind has kinda gotten used to it. That was the way it was. I missed hearing her breathing, and getting up in the night, shuffling around in the dark. Some nights she prayed way up in the night, thanking God for all manner of things and asking His blessing and begging His forgiveness; Guessed, maybe, I missed that a little, too. All the time I was thinking about Vivian, the rest of my mind was smoothing out. My legs ached from tiredness and my eyes were heavy. I stuck one hand down in my pocket until my fingers touched the pistol. I tugged my protection out and eased it down by my right side. Off in the distance, deep in the night, a train whistle moaned low and lonesome and the scent of honeysuckle drifted on the sweet evening breeze.

Twenty-eight

THE SMELL OF PERCOLATING coffee woke me. I sat up, stretched, and glanced around.

Gives a man a strange sensation to wake up and find a Shetland pony staring at him. This one was shaggy, black and white, and looked blind in one eye. He snorted at me and I nodded and got to my feet. I bent over and picked up the blanket and the pistol. Jamming the pistol into a pants pocket, I slung the blanket across one shoulder and walked around behind the shed and into the woods where I took care of business. On the way back, I stopped and stroked the pony's muzzle.

Daylight hadn't quite made it as I strolled up the slope though the blue promise of morning. Coffee aromas grew stronger the closer I got to the house. Sparrows had nested under the eaves and I could hear baby birds chirping.

In the first pale light of day, the house appeared even more ramshackedly. Paint was peeling off the wooden slats and there weren't screens on any of the windows. A shallow porch ran across the back and a hound sprawled on the floor of the porch. He opened one eye and stared at me without moving. A wringer washer stood in one corner and a couple of straight back chairs were pushed against the back wall of the house. The back door was squarely in the middle of the porch and I climbed the three steps and walked across the porch, keeping one eye on the dog.

I knocked on the door and in a moment it swung open. A hatchet-faced woman wearing a sleeveless dress peered out at me. Her eyes had a yellowish cast and her nose was bird-beaky. Flour dusted her hands. A strong aroma of coffee drifted out the door, and I could smell biscuits baking. In the corner of the kitchen I could see from the porch, an old lady sat in a rocking chair, a shawl draped around both shoulders. Her kinky hair looked like gray wool.

"Tobias home?" I asked the sharp-nosed woman.

She wiped her hands on her apron, turned and walked out of the kitchen. Seconds later, I heard her calling out the boy's name. Over in her corner, the old woman rocked steadily, black eyes glittering, chewing on something. I wondered if it was a hunk of meat or a plug of tobacco.

Heavy footsteps sounded in the hall and then Tyree's uncle stepped around the corner, stooping as he stepped through the low hanging door, swinging his arms, then lifting them above his head. He was bare chested and the muscles rippled under his black skin like restless snakes.

"Morning," he said.

"Morning. Tyree up?"

"Just woke him. Boy's got to rub the sleep out of his eyes and put his britches on. Be along shortly. Wanna come in?"

"I'll wait out here," I said. Being in a kitchen with a couple of colored women wasn't what I wanted this early in the morning.

"Coffee be ready in a minute. You want a cup?" He grinned at me. "Got a long walk ahead of you. Cup of coffee won't harm you none."

"Well..."

"All right then. Wait out on the porch and I'll bring it to you."

I turned and slow-walked to the edge of the porch. Off in the woods, daylight was painting the tops of the trees and birds swirled up out of the canopy, winging skyward and calling out to one another. There were red birds and brown birds and black birds and birds with shiny heads and birds with green and blue feathers, birds as big as chickens, and birds so small they were no more than wedges whirling across the sky. The morning seemed alive with birds.

"Quite a sight, ain't it, mister?"

"Never saw anything like it before. And I've been a lot of places, too."

"Here's your coffee."

"Smells mighty good."

"First cup's always the best, I say."

The cup was warm in my hands. The aroma was powerful. My stomach gurgled as I raised the cup and sipped. The coffee was strong and black, flavored with chicory. It burned down my throat and into my stomach.

"Damn," I said.

Tyree's uncle grinned and sipped gingerly at his coffee. "Warms you right up, don't it?"

We stood there on that creaky old porch, sipping coffee and watching the sun come up and the birds tracking patterns I could almost see in the pale blue sky. Chatter came to us from the kitchen, muted and distorted, more sounds than words, but comforting in a certain way. I'm no

Biblical scholar, but it seemed to me a little like it must have felt to stand in the Garden of Eden watching the very first morning being born.

Drifting across the cool air were the smells of bacon frying and aftershave and the warm smell of animals and wood burning. Running through them all was the scent of my own stale sweat and unwashed body. Smelling that sweat brought back the night before.

"Can I ask you a question?"

"Sure. What you want to know?"

I pulled my billfold out and slipped the photograph out. In the daylight you could tell it had passed through dozens of hands. Gladys still smiled, though, and, despite the rough night, she looked real pretty. Even now I couldn't deny that. I handed over the picture.

"Ever seen this woman?"

He studied the photo. Studied it good. I'd have bet cash money that if he ever did see her, he'd know her right off.

"No, don't believe I've ever seen this woman. Should I have?"

"No reason you would have. Just thought I'd ask."

"Why you looking for her? That is, if you don't mind my asking."

"Nope, don't mind one bit." A hawk flew out of the trees and I watched him wing his way across the yard. I followed him until the sky swallowed him. Someday that sky, or the earth, or a river somewhere would swallow me, too. Everybody gets swallowed, sooner or later. Wasn't pretty to think about it, but then the truth often leans ugly. Even though I'd never been the sharpest tack in the box, I'd learned that much. Learned it the hard way.

"Let's say I owe her something and I'm a man who likes to pay his debts."

Tyree's uncle gave me a cutting glance and he acted like he was fixing to say something. Only, he didn't—simply turned his head and spat into the yard.

"If you ever do see her, will you let me know?"

"Sounds like she's important to you."

"Yeah, but not that way."

He stared off into the morning. After a moment, his eyes changed. "So that's how it is, huh?"

"That's how it is," I said. "Purely some unfinished business I need to take care of." My eyes felt gritty and I rubbed at them. "She's liable to be with a man. If he's got a scar shaped like a fishhook right on the tip end of his jaw bone you'll know for certain they're the ones I'm searching for."

Tyree's uncle nodded and rubbed the side of his face. I could hear the stubble rustling. "I'll let you know," he said.

Laughter rose in the kitchen, cackles like a couple of Rhode Island Reds who had both laid an egg. Thinking of eggs made me realize how hungry I was; I tried to remember when I'd eaten last. All I could recall about the night before was drinking a lot of beer and smoking cigarettes I'd bummed off men a touch drunker. Maybe I'd eaten a few boiled peanuts, but they were hardly true food. Which would make the chicken the boy and I had eaten on the other side of the bayou at noon the day before the last solid food I'd had. No wonder my guts were growling.

"Them women, they're something else," Tobias said. "Always cutting up, acting silly, laughing one minute, then crying the next."

I took another sip of coffee. "What makes them act like that?"

The big man shrugged. "Simply being women, I reckon."

The women cackled again, then one of them shrieked. The shrill noise made my head hurt.

"How do you stand that all day?"

Tobias chuckled. "I don't. If I don't have work, I go putter in my garden, or squirrel hunting, or go fishing. Failing that, I find some of the fellas and sit around and shoot the breeze. Maybe sip on a little shine, if anybody has some."

"Doesn't sound like a bad life."

"Oh, it's not. Not at all."

The coffee was cooler now and I took a bigger sip. I could feel it working on my nerves, bringing me to life.

"What sort of work you do?"

"I'm a brick mason when there's that work available. I'm also a pretty fair house painter and not a half-bad carpenter, if I say so myself. When there ain't nothing else, I'll cut cane or work a little in the timber. Whatever I can do to make a dollar. Got a game leg, sure, but that don't stop a determined man. Used to hang around the house feeling sorry for myself. Then, I saved up and got me an operation from a white doctor over to Montreaux and ever since then I've been getting stronger." He glanced at me over the rim of his cup. "What about you?"

The question caught me off guard and I sipped at my coffee to give me a minute to think. Across the backyard, the pony was stomping and snorting. Sunlight covered the yard in pale yellow. The air was still cool, but the day already had that hot smell.

"Sorta between jobs right now." I drained the last of my coffee. "At one time, I used to be in the banking business."

Maybe the man believed me; maybe he didn't. Those words weren't totally a lie. Nobody ever tells the truth anyway. Not all the way. I cut a look at him out of the corners of my eyes, but he was peering out across the morning, his gaze on the timber, or beyond. I wondered what he was thinking.

After a moment, he turned toward me and grinned.

"Don't know about you, mister, but I'm getting hungry." He nodded in the direction of the kitchen. "Come on in and eat with us. The boy should be about ready by now."

"I don't know. I mean..."

"Aw, come on. Them women won't kill you. Besides, a little fatback and eggs will do you good. Put some meat on your bones. No offense, but you look a mite peaked to me."

I started to say something more, but my guts were growling so loud I knew he could hear them, so I simply shrugged and followed the man inside.

Twenty-nine

TYREE AND FOUR OR FIVE other yard apes sat around the table. A couple more, a year or two older, stood. All were stuffing biscuits and meat in their mouths. Everyone looked up when I stepped into the kitchen. Floorboards sagged beneath me as I watched the expressions on the faces of the boys change. I felt like I was a man who dropped out of the clouds. Tyree grinned.

"'Morning, Mr. Ray."

"How you doing, Tyree?"

"Doing fine, Mr. Ray. Only plenty good and hungry."

I nodded. "Could stand to eat myself."

Tobias waved his hands like he was shooing flies. "Here now, you boys scatter. This man and I need some room. We got a day ahead of us, and a man has to have proper nourishment. Besides, you all stay to the table, you'll hog every last bite. Now get. Shoo."

He tugged a chair out and motioned with his hands. "Sit down, here, mister. Lenora, fetch this man a plate and some of them hot biscuits. My wife makes the best biscuits in all of

Louisiana. Everybody says so. Here's your plate. Now fill it up. Meat's pretty good, too. Lots of fat, for sure, and fat is what gives meat flavor, 'specially pig meat."

It had been a long time since I'd been in a kitchen like this. All the children running around and the steam and the smells and the biscuits heaped up on a plate. It was almost too much. I hated to eat like some wild animal and made myself fold my hands and put them in my lap.

"All those kids yours?" I asked.

"Well," he said, "not strictly. That is, they is and they ain't."

I must have looked puzzled, 'cause he said, "Let me explain." He picked up a biscuit and broke it and poured molasses out of a chipped bowl over the halves. "Good stuff, black strap molasses. Best thing in the world with biscuits. You want some?" He waggled the bowl at me.

"I'm good, but thanks."

"Anyway, about those kids. For some reason only He knows, the good Lord decided not to bless me and Lenora with any children of our own. He knows best, of course, but we surely did pray and weep over her barrenness. Then, almost five years ago, He began to reveal His plan. There was a family lived along Burnham Creek, 'bout two miles south of town. Hurricane blew up that September and the rain, oh my, the rain. You never saw such rain. Rained for three days and three nights and they was lots of folks was wondering if God had changed His mind and was going to give us forty days and nights of it." Tobias forked biscuit into his mouth, and I ate some myself while he chewed. Had to admit it was tasty.

"Damn, that's good stuff," he said, swallowing and grinning like a huge black possum. Lenora, she sure can cook." He winked at me. "Women likes to hear words like that. Anyhoo, to make a long story short, that Burnham Creek flashed up out of its banks, and killed the father and one of the young'uns. Never did find the mother. Figure the creek carried her way far away. Who knows, maybe clear to the Gulf. The two that was left didn't have no kin, least that they or anybody else knew of, and they needed a place to stay. And, here was me and Lenora with an empty nest." He shrugged.

"That's how it all started. One after another, orphans, runaways, abandoned kiddos, they all ended up here with us. Church of God down the road helps out. Gives us the fifth Sunday collections. What's more, several of the rich folks in town send food and used clothing along right regular. Plus, lots of people who ain't got hardly nothing gives whatever they can. A couple of eggs say, or a dime, or some school books they don't need no longer."

"You must be right proud," I said.

"Oh, don't know about proud," he said, leaning back in his chair and dabbing at his mouth with a napkin. "Happy, maybe. Happier than I've ever been in my life." He inclined his head toward me. Lines were carved into his face like grooves that form in worn leather. "Man don't always know what'll make him happy. Sometimes he's certain it's one thing, only it turns out to be something else entirely. Life's sure funny that way."

He shook his head. "No sir, mister, you can trust old Tobias Williams on that. Man don't ever really know until it happens to him. Sometimes what will truly make him happy comes smooth and easy, other times it's rougher than a pissed off porcupine."

I didn't say anything. Only forked another piece of meat into my mouth and eased back in my chair. For a moment, I closed my eyes and let the warmth from the stove and the dull murmur of voices flow over me like a slow brown river. And it was like back before the Crash, when I'd come in off the road and sit in the old farmhouse kitchen with Mom and Dad, rocking in the rocking chair that always sat in front of the west window, scratching old Jack's ears, sensing my mind emptying and then filling up again, only this time with peace. I wondered if I'd ever find that peace of mind again.

Thirty

THE SUN HAD GONE down behind the line of trees and taken the heat of the day with it. Earlier, there had been a breeze, but it had died off and the afternoon had gone quiet. You could smell the bayou – the stagnant water and dead fish and damp earth, and feel the sweat trickle down your back, and hear the mosquitoes whine and woodpeckers hammering on dead sycamores. The boy was a few feet ahead of me. His shadow fell on the ground and I stepped on it with every stride. I didn't recognize the terrain and wondered how many more miles we still had to journey.

As though he'd read my mind, the boy looked over his shoulder and said, "See that big dead sycamore up there? The one's that's all hollow inside."

"Sure."

"Once we get there, we turn north and it's only about three more miles." Tyree grinned. Three miles must not matter much to him, I figured.

"Damn long walk to town, kid. Why don't you guys move closer?"

Tyree shrugged. “Don’t know. Never thought about it.”

“Does your mother ever talk about moving? After all, you guys are sure in a lonesome place. Bet the nearest neighbor’s not within five miles.”

The boy shook his head. “You’d lose, Mister Ray. If you cut through the fields, Old Man Tompkins’ place ain’t more than two and a half, maybe three miles.”

“Maybe,” I said, “but you all are still a long way from civilization.”

The boy laughed and walked on. I pushed on after him. Without another word, we strolled on through the fading gold of the afternoon. My legs were tired, but it was that good tired your muscles get when you’ve been on a hike, or plowed a field, or walked a long way to check on a sick neighbor. Not like the tiredness that settles in your bones when you’re on the run.

However, when you thought about the whole picture, I was still on the run. On the run from John Law if he ever placed me at any of those bank jobs, on the run from Johnny and Gladys, and on the run from all the other demons that were only a step or two behind me. Not that I could have described them. See, I’d never stopped running long enough to check out their faces.

Thirty-one

THE AIR WAS GOING PURPLE when we stepped out of the stand of live oaks. The shanty reared up before us. Clean clothes hung on the clothesline and smoke curled from the chimney. Leroy was sitting on a stump in the yard, his face turned toward the line of trees that rose behind us. As I watched, he jumped up and ran on his bird legs into the house. Seconds later, the woman came out and stood in the yard staring in our direction.

"Appears your mom's spotted us," I said.

"Yeah," the boy said. "That Leroy, he run and told her, dang him. Was hoping to surprise her."

"She'll be glad to see you," I said.

"You, too," the boy said. Then he hung his head and scuffed at the dirt with his toes. "She thinks you're a real nice man."

I laughed and punched him lightly on the shoulder. "You'd better learn now, boy, that you can't always believe everything a woman tells you. Not even your mother."

He laughed at that and looked over at me sorta mischievous like. Then he took off running waving and hollering at his mommy. She whooped and waved right back at him, and I know it was silly – it must have been my sentimental day – but for a moment it seemed like she was waving at me and I was her old man coming home after a long journey. Without thinking further, I waved back. Then I laughed at myself, figuring all that fever had burnt up an important piece of my brain.

I slowed my pace and watched the boy run on ahead. A boy misses his momma. Still missed mine ever now and then. At the edge of the field, I kicked up a covey of quail and they rose with a whirling of wings. I watched them become one with the encroaching darkness. When they had disappeared, I pulled a pack of cigarettes I'd bought in town out of my shirt pocket and shook one out. Striking a match, I fired it up and drew smoke into my lungs. The air was cooler now and the frogs had started up, and it was pleasant to lean against a fence post and smoke a cigarette. A man gets so busy at times that he forgets what really makes him feel good. Something small rustled in the tall grass along the fencerow, but the light was too chancy to tell for certain what creature it was.

Twilight blanketed the yard. Oil lamps burned inside the shanty by the time I got within rock throwing distance. Out of nowhere, I had the strongest urge to have a dog, one that would come bounding out to greet me when I came in of the evening. Didn't have to be a special dog, no pureblood, simply a friendly old dog. Back when I was a kid, I'd had dogs. But that had been a long time ago and things were different now. Lots of things were different now. I slogged on across the yard.

When I stepped in out of the twilight, the woman was at the stove, stirring something in a big kettle and she turned with a spoon in her hand. Sweat glistened on her round face. In the short time I'd been gone I'd almost forgotten how fat and black she was.

"Are you hungry? I fixed you and Tyree a big pot of soup beans. Want a bowl? I've done dished Tyree up."

"What about you and Leroy?"

"Oh, we ate a while ago. They's plenty of beans. Cooked enough to feed the entire congregation."

"All right," I said. "I'll take a bowl."

"Good. Now you just sit down and I'll fetch them beans to you. Know you have to be about plum tuckered out. That's a long walk."

"Oh, I'm okay," I said as I sat down. Didn't tell her, but it did feel good to take a load off my feet. Back when I'd been robbing banks, I'd been doing a whole lot more riding in a car than walking and my feet were hot and sore. A blister was coming on one heel and I was glad I'd thought to buy me a half-pint in town. Booze and cigarettes might not number among life's essentials, but they sure as hell helped a man get through the rough patches.

"Tyree said you spent the night with my brother."

I had to laugh at that. The woman arched her eyebrows at me. I shook my head. "Spent the night in the pony shed."

"Didn't he ask you inside?"

"Yeah, he asked."

"Then why did you sleep out with the horses?"

"Didn't want to sleep inside, I suppose."

Out of the corner of my eye, I could see her giving me the fish-eye. "Too many kids around for me," I said and closed my eyes. Hadn't realized how tired I was. 'Course I hadn't slept all that well the night before. If I hadn't been worried about hurting her feelings I'd have gone right on to bed. Instead, I rested my eyes for a moment.

Maybe I dozed off. I'll admit to drifting. The smell of hot beans drew me back into the room.

"You want some cornbread to go with the beans?"

She had a kind voice. Had to give her that. Probably, she was a nice person. But for some reason she got on my nerves.

"That would be good."

I could hear her moving around across the room. I concentrated on eating my beans. I was hungrier than I'd realized. The bowl was half empty before the woman got the cornbread to the table. I nodded my thanks. She hovered around me like a soft dark cloud. I could smell her body. It wasn't unpleasant. Essentially a musky, animal scent.

"Here's your cornbread. Fresh made. Should go mighty fine with those beans."

"Thanks."

"You're welcome, mister."

"Just call me Ray," I said around a mouthful of beans. Don't know why I said that. Why should I tell that fat colored woman my name? Especially since she'd quit asking. Maybe it was the hot beans and cornbread. Been a long time since any woman had been nice to me. Maybe I was getting soft. Getting gunshot and fighting fever surely affects a man.

Her hand pressed against my good shoulder. It was heavy, yet, at the same time, warm and soft. I picked up the cornbread and bit off one corner. It was still warm from the oven. I'd eaten steakmeat that didn't taste half as good.

"You can cook some good cornbread, woman."

"My momma taught me. She was the best cook. Oh, you ought to have seen her pies. Meringue three inches high and so pretty they looked like a painting."

"My mother used to cook pies, too. Only no meringue. Hers were berry pies."

"What kind of berries?"

"Blackberry and gooseberry, I remember. But it was her raspberry pies I liked best. Dad used to have raspberry canes out in one corner of the garden." I spooned more beans in my mouth. "But that was before the Crash and all the Hoovervilles and before the banks started closing in on the little man, then closing him down."

"I heard tell that man Hoover caused the hard times. Is that right, Ray?"

She hesitated on my name. No more than a heartbeat, but enough to notice. It sounded strange to hear a grown woman other than Gladys say my name. A colored gal at that. Still, she had a pleasant voice, even if she did drag her words out. Funny, but I didn't mind her saying it as much as I'd figured I would. Guess everybody likes to hear their name spoken by another, makes them feel as if the amount to that much, anyway. Probably a man likes hearing a woman say his name the best. Before, I'd thought for sure it would make me sick hearing some old mammy say my name, but when it happened it wasn't so bad. Life can sure surprise you. Learned that lesson the hard way, more than once.

"He sure didn't help matters," I said, "but I reckon plenty of others played a part."

I broke off a hunk of cornbread and jammed it in my mouth. As I chewed, I closed my eyes. Riding all alone for three days in a boxcar, like I had plenty of times, a man learns right enough how to pretend.

Everybody pretends, one time or another, one way or another. Life was absolutely too hard to get through without pretending. I ate my beans and cornbread while I pretended I was going to get up from the table and walk outside and shoot Johnny and Gladys right between the eyes.

"You want some more beans, Ray? More cornbread?"

I shivered. Way she said my name, she'd be calling me honey, or baby next. Enough to scare a sinner straight.

"No," I said, "but if we've got any coffee, would you heat me up a cup? I'm going to go out in the yard and have me a smoke."

She said something, but I was scooting my chair back and patting my pockets down for the cigarettes, not paying attention. Her eyes were on me. Could sense that. In my mind, they felt hot and heavy. Like warm tar. But I ignored them, and her, and started walking toward the door.

Thirty-two

DARKNESS COVERED THE YARD. Under the live oaks the air was black. A few stars had popped out, but the moon was missing in action. Down along the bayou the frogs had started up. My eyes were beginning to grow used to the night and I picked my way across the yard. At the edge of the yard was a stump, worn smooth by the wind, and the rain, and the years. Whatever kind of tree that had stood there had been a big one. Two grown people could have sat on it, maybe three. I sat down on the stump, tapped out another cigarette and struck a match against the stump.

The night was quiet, heavy, and soft. There was no wind and even the birds were still. Only sounds were the frogs croaking, and, now and then, the whine of a mosquito. The backs of my legs ached and I puffed on the cigarette and tried not to think about anything.

For a while that worked. Then I remembered one time when Gladys and I had sat outside in the dark on a quiet night like this. We'd been in Kentucky and the car had broken down outside Lexington on some back road that ran between horse farms and lines of maples that had been huge before either of us had been born. If memory served, it had been called Old Frankfort Pike.

Johnny had walked off to try and find help, and Gladys and I had crossed the road and climbed over a stone fence slaves must have built. Beyond the fence the ground had sloped gently upward, as though some giant had rolled it up as a joke. Flowers and tall grasses covered that ground and we had held hands and climbed to the top of that knoll. All the stars in the universe seemed to have been visible that night and we had stretched out on our backs and stared up at them, trying to find the Big Dipper, and Venus, and Orion.

That night had been so quiet I could hear Gladys breathing softly, and, after a few minutes, I'd quit looking up at the stars and started looking at her. In the pale starlight, I could see her chest rising and falling, and then she had turned to me and our lips had met and our fingers had gotten very busy. Gladys was always pretty, but I truly don't believe I ever saw her look more beautiful than that night when she lay naked and smooth in the Kentucky starlight.

"You awful quiet tonight, Mr. Ray."

"Hey, Tyree, what you doing out here? You about scared me to death."

"Didn't you hear me coming?"

"Nope. Was thinking about old times."

"I do that sometimes, but Momma she gets on me. Says I'm daydreaming."

I took a drag and blew smoke out into darkness. A dog had started barking somewhere off to the east, down along the bayou, and I figured coon hunters were out. "Daydreaming never hurt, at least if a fella doesn't overdo it."

Movement caught my eye and I turned and watched the woman step out of the shanty and start across the yard. The little one was tagging along. Tyree put his hand on my shoulder. I took another hit off the cigarette. I couldn't hear the dog anymore.

"Tyree, what you doing out here? Thought I told you to get your brother ready for bed."

"Just talking to Mr. Ray, Momma."

"Well, tell him good night and get on in that bed. You've had a big adventure and a long walk. Know your poor body has to be plum wore out."

"Ah, I ain't really tired," Tyree said, stifling a yawn.

Before his mother could say anything, I patted him on the butt. "Mind your momma now, boy. Once I finish this cigarette, I'm going to turn in myself. We both walked a lot of miles the last couple of days and I don't know about you, but I didn't sleep so good in that old pony barn."

"All right," he said as he took his brother's hand. The woman and I watched them walk across the yard and into the house. The dog had started up again and it sounded like he had one treed.

"That Tyree, he's a good one. If he stays straight, he'll make a good man."

"They're both good boys."

I puffed on my cigarette and held the smoke in my mouth for a long time. Finally, I let it out slow, like air seeping out of a slow leak in a tire.

"Well, I'd say that's right."

That old dog was really going now. Other dogs joined in. Sounded like there were three of them, maybe four. All my life I'd heard men talk about going coon hunting. I'd never been.

"Care if I sit down with you, Ray?"

"Reckon it's more your stump than mine," I said, and scooted over a few inches. Like I said, it was a big stump, but she was a big woman. Her body pressed softly against mine. She was soft all over. I didn't say a word. She didn't either. The dogs kept on barking, but the sounds grew fainter.

Suddenly she laughed and the sound was loud in the night and it startled me.

"What's so funny?"

"Was just thinking that I ain't never sat on a stump in the dark with no white man before."

"What a hell of a thing to say."

"Well, it's the truth. I'm only telling the truth."

"Just 'cause it's the truth don't mean you have to say it."

She laughed again. "No need for you to worry, mister. It's pitch dark out here. Nobody will ever see us."

"I'm not worried."

Her fingers brushed across the back of my neck. "What are you then?"

I ground the cigarette out against the stump and turned around to face her. There was something I wanted to say. Something clever that would shut her up.

Only her face was closer than I expected and it glistened in the starlight like a dark moon. Her lips were full and soft looking and I don't know why, maybe I was overtired or the fever had come back on me, but I put my arms around her and kissed her right on the mouth. And she kissed me right back and it was a sweet kiss. I sat there stunned, knowing I'd gone crazy in the night. What if my folks had seen me, or another white man? Kissing a colored woman, my God, oh my God.

Right then is when I should have jumped up and wiped my mouth and spit it clean. But I didn't. I told myself it was because I was tired. I told myself it was because the woman had been nice to me and I didn't want to hurt her feelings. I told myself it was purely because I was lonely. And I guess there were slivers of truth in all those reasons. But the bigger truth was that I sat there and kept on kissing her because I wanted to.

The fact that she was fat and black as hot tar didn't bother me much right then. The night was warm and quiet, and she was soft and willing, and we kept on kissing. After a while my hands got to roving.

She pulled back then. "Let's go inside. It's more comfortable in a bed." She was whispering and her breath was warm against my ear. I had to strain to understand her words. I could feel my heart beating inside my chest. Felt like something small and alive had crawled in there.

"What about the boys?"

"They'll be asleep."

"Won't they wake up?"

"Tyree's got to be dead tired after all that walking and Leroy will stay right in the bed if Tyree's there. Besides, I'll be in my bed before daylight."

"Well..."

"Come on, Ray. You know you want to, and I want to, too. What's wrong with two people grabbing a few minutes of happiness?"

While I was trying to think up an answer, she pressed her lips against mine and it was like I was being slowly eaten alive, and I thought about one time I saw a man down in Florida feed a rabbit to this python he owned and the damn rabbit was alive. Gave me nightmares for a week. I'd been roofing a barn for the man.

Then she leaned back and I could see that she'd undone the top three buttons to her dress when I wasn't paying attention and her breasts were hanging loose. In the starlight they looked like cantaloupe that had been through a fire and come out intact, only blackened.

She put my hands in hers and guided them to her breasts. They were soft and warm and I squeezed them gently. Then I bent my neck and kissed them with only my lips and the very tip of my tongue.

"Let's go inside," she whispered. I kissed her breasts one more time, then nodded. We pushed off the stump and started walking across the yard. Halfway there, I felt her hand slip into mine. At the doorway, I thought about Gladys and how in all the years we'd been together I'd never been untrue to her. Never really thought twice about another woman, if you want to know the truth. But then I remembered where all that faithfulness had gotten me and I squeezed Vivian's hand and followed her through the door.

Thirty-three

DEEP IN THE NIGHT, I swirled awake with warm breath caressing my neck. Through the semi-darkness, I gazed down on the woman curled against me. A late moon had risen and shafts of moonlight poured through the open door. Enough of it drifted across the room to highlight her face and body.

We were naked, and with her black as Kentucky coal and me the color of fresh milk, we looked a touch strange. She was fat, too. Rolls of it hung around her waist and her thighs were thicker than mine. But, remembering the sweetness of her loving, I found it easy to forgive all her faults and shortcomings. As if I was somebody special who could judge anybody. Ha. What a joke. I said me a quick little prayer, in case anybody out there was listening. Then I bent my head and kissed her closed eyes and pulled her body tighter to mine.

Lying there half-asleep, I wondered how I'd feel when daylight came. Things often have a way of taking on a different shape in the daylight; maybe I'd hate her, or myself, or both of us. But this was the night, and I was a lonely man, and she was a lonely woman. Besides, in the middle of a hot quiet night, color didn't seem to matter all that much.

For what seemed like hours, I stayed awake, thinking over many things, worrying them in my mind, glancing down at her now and then, as though to assure myself that she was still there. Which was crazy, because I could feel her soft weight sagging against my body. In a way I couldn't put into words, that weight felt good, and I smiled. On the other hand, hypocrite that I was, I felt grateful no one else was there to see us lying as one.

Sometime, I guess it must have been three o'clock or so—it had that dead of the night feeling—I closed my eyes and scrunched down in the bed as best I could, making myself comfortable against her. Frogs were still croaking and I could hear cattle lowing in the night, and then, way off in the distance—so faint it sounded like the after effects of a dream, I heard a train whistle, long and low and sounding as lonesome as lost feels. I thought of all the trains I'd run to catch, and the ones I'd caught, and the ones I'd missed. When the train had moved on down the line, I got to wondering about what I was going to do next, and what was going to happen to me, and if I'd ever see Gladys or Johnny or the old home place back in Platte County.

My eyes were growing heavier, and I could sense my mind starting to drift toward the nothingness of sleep, but before I let go of the sweet, rare night, I said her name. Said it soft, but clear, like a small bell ringing. Remember that as clear as Christmas morning.

Thirty-four

MY SHOULDER WAS healing. The nerves and arteries and muscles and whatever else made up a man's shoulder now moved smoothly After more than a month of dabbing with peroxide at the hole the bullet had made, and washing around it good, and keeping it bandaged with strips cut from an old sheet, the bullet hole had scabbed over. Old Ray was eating pretty high on the hog, too. The woman could sure cook; that I had to give her. People had started bringing in food, too, after my trip to town. It was as if I'd passed some test and was now at least a partially accepted member of some unincorporated community. That sense of belonging made me feel funny. Since Dad had lost the farm, I'd not belonged anywhere. But that funny feeling didn't stop me from eating the pork chops, and the fish, and the eggs Vivian's cousins, nephews, and friends brought in.

Strength was seeping back into my body, too, the way an underground spring will seep up to the surface when the soil and rocks lay right. Some days I worked in the garden for an hour, or more.

I was smarter now, or at least I'd learnt a lesson, because I worked either before the sun grew strong or after the shadows of afternoon began to fall. Not being able to do what I wanted to, when I wanted to still aggravated me, but I figured by the end of summer I'd be close to normal.

Most mornings before breakfast, I stuck the pistol in my pocket and walked down to where the bayou made a great curling bend. Inside the curl was a meadow filled with daises, milk weeds, and a sawtooth grass that came to my knees. Patches of clover grew there and wild flowers with blossoms no bigger than a fingernail, and as blue as a cloudless October sky. At the far end of the meadow, earth was mounded up as though at some point, say a million years ago, the earth had spasmed. A number of large rocks and fallen trees were lodged against the base of the mound and I sat empty bottles and tin cans on them for target practice. I'd never earn a marksman badge, but I was getting better every time I shot.

Dew still dampened the grass this morning, while daylight was struggling to work its way through the timber. I was shooting at a Coca-Cola bottle I'd found washed up on the bayou mudflats. My first shot had been high and left. Second one had been dead on, only six inches low. Squinting against the light, I took a deep breath, held it and let it out. I squeezed the trigger. Glass shattered and I smiled.

"You're getting good at that shooting."

I jerked and whirled around. Been so locked in on hitting the bottle that I'd had no idea anyone was behind me.

"What are you doing here?"

"Seen you head out lots of mornings and got to wondering what you were doing. Figured I knew though. Heard the shooting, you know."

"What gives you any right to spy on me?"

"I'm not spying. This here ain't your land. Reckon I've got as much right on it as you do. Maybe more."

I shrugged. "You didn't have to sneak up on me."

"I didn't sneak up on you," the woman said. "Been standing here at least five minutes watching you shoot. You sure are intense." She rubbed the palm of one hand along my cheek. "You aiming to shoot someone?"

I let my eyes drift away from her, off toward the bayou. Buzzards floated above the tree canopy. For a week, the sky had been the color of pewter, the sun boiling across it. By now this day's sun had crested the trees and heat shimmers were forming.

"Might come a time, Vivian, when I have to." I let my eyes journey back to her face. In the morning light, her blackness bordered on purple. Her face shone like a freshly washed eggplant. Maybe it was my imagination, but there seemed to be a worried cast to her eyes.

"Sometimes folks don't leave a man any choice."

She dapped at her sweaty face with a man's handkerchief. "You talking about shooting them that shot you, ain't you?"

"If they don't see me first, I expect it will come to that."

"Why did they shoot you, Ray? Are you in trouble?"

"Not with the law. Least not that I know of." I looked off toward the bayou again. A white egret was mincing down the bank. Sunlight spread hot on my face. Didn't see how anyone could stand up all day to that sun.

"Let's say, though that I've been through some bad times. Dark times, you might call 'em. I'm not proud of them, not proud of everything I've done. But I swear I ain't all bad, and, for sure, I'm not the same man as I was back then." Exactly what had changed me, I didn't share. Simply let my words linger in the still air.

The woman shaded her eyes with a hand, putting me in mind of a painting I'd once seen in a museum. "You one of them what's been robbing banks, ain't you?"

I didn't say anything. What was there to say? A woodpecker had started up, hammering like he was aiming to join a band. On the far side of the mounded earth, a bull bellowed and the faint hum of bees among the clover drifted through the morning air.

"Well, just cause you done something bad once, don't mean you have to keep on doing bad things. Ray, you know every bit as well as I do that ain't a solitary one of us perfect. Only perfect man who ever lived is dead. Crucified a long time ago by jealous men. Didn't do them no good. They tortured Him, then killed Him afore burying Him in a tomb. Whole bunch of them rolled a great huge rock in front of that tomb so His followers couldn't give him a decent Christian burial. Only all of that never did them one ounce of good. See, the angel of the Lord came down and rolled the stone away and sweet Jesus rose on the third day and ascended into Heaven, where He lives with God the Father."

The woman paused and stepped closer. She smelled faintly of cinnamon and flour and sweat. Her eyes shimmered like pools of fresh oil. They swept across my face. She was trembling ever so slightly, and I wondered if that was on account of the heat. Or the talking about God. Lots of folks, 'specially women, get right worked up about their religion. She licked her lips. Part of me wanted to kiss them.

"Jesus died for our sins, Ray. For yours, and for mine, and for whoever it was what shot you. All you have to do is ask for His forgiveness and profess Him and you'll be saved in that very drawing of breath. Then you can forgive, too. Turn all that ugly hatred out of your heart and let the past be the past. Just 'cause you've lived one way, don't mean you can't change and live another." She smiled at me, real sweet like and kinda shy, and in that moment in the morning, she was a young girl. She reached out and put one hand on my bare right arm. At the end of that arm was the gun. It felt heavy.

"Why don't you give me the gun, Ray? I'll keep it safe for you."

For a few seconds I didn't say anything. Then I reached with my free hand and, as gently as I could, pried her fingers from my gun arm. "You go on back home, baby," I said. "I'll be along soon."

"But, Ray," she said, and, sensing she was fixing to say more, I kissed her mouth shut. Surely I had a bad case of sun poisoning, kissing a colored woman in broad daylight. Maybe I had gone a touch loco, too, what with Johnny and Gladys double-crossing me and then getting shot and catching that fever. Still, no matter what anyone might think or say, the woman had been nice to me. Nicer than anybody had been in a mighty long time. Something was inside me that didn't want to hurt her. Even though I knew that, sooner or later, I almost surely would.

She put her arms around me and hugged me and I hugged her back, and all the time I was hearing that woodpecker pounding hell out of a tree, and thinking about Gladys with Johnny.

Finally, I bent and kissed both her checks. I could taste salt and I wondered if that was from sweat, or from tears. She sniffed a couple of times, then drifted her fingertips across my face before she turned and started plodding back toward the shanty, walking as though she was bearing an awful burden. And maybe she was. Hard to say what's in another's heart.

Perhaps she turned and waved, but if she did, I never knew because I'd already turned and aimed the gun at a patch of bare earth about a quarter way up the mound. Staring at that bare black earth, I could see the silhouette of Gladys' face etched in the dirt, and I squinted, took in a deep breath, then let it out real slow. When it was all expelled, I squeezed the trigger as gently as if I was crooking the finger of a baby.

Thirty-five

TYREE AND I WERE hoeing corn when I heard the jaybird start up. Bird was squawking like his tail feathers were on fire. I glanced up, but didn't see anything unusual and went back to hoeing.

A couple of minutes later, Tyree elbowed me. "Someone's coming." He was pointing across the cornfield. I followed the line of sight on past the house and into the scrub pines beyond. Birds, disturbed by someone, or something, circled above the trees. I nodded and we leaned on our hoe handles and waited.

After a few seconds, a man stepped out of the tree line. Something in his walk was familiar.

"Looks like Uncle Tobias," the boy said.

"Does he come out here often?"

Tyree shrugged. "Not too often, 'cause of his leg, but every now and then. Mostly he comes when he can a ride the biggest part of the way. He likes to check on Mom, specially since Dad, well, you know."

"Sure," I said, "I understand." A butterfly fluttered around Tyree. It circled him twice before it landed on his arm. It was small, even for a butterfly, and its wings were blue. "Reckon we better go and see what's up."

Tyree nodded, slung his hoe up over his shoulder, and started back for the house. I watched the butterfly drift into the next row of cornstalks. Then I picked up my hoe and followed the kid.

Tobias and Vivian were sitting around the table next to the stove. Leroy was on his uncle's knee sucking on a candy cane. A bag of horehound candy sat in the middle of the table. Everybody looked up as Tyree and I stepped through the door. I nodded at Tobias. He lifted a hand.

Vivian was asking him something about a cousin who'd been sick. The cousin's name was Maydean, and apparently there was something wrong with her heart. "Hear everybody at the Freewill is praying for her. Is she any better?"

Tobias shook his head. "Don't seem to be, Viv. Keeps on having chest pains, and Johnny Liston told me she fainted dead away twice last week."

"Blood must not be flowing good. She's been sick for a long time now, ain't she?"

Tobias studied the ceiling. "Most two years, I reckon."

"How old you think Maydean is?"

"Must be getting on for fifty. She's a few years older than I am, and I'll be forty-five the tenth of next month."

He glanced at me, and Vivian caught the look and pressed her lips together. Then she smiled. "Tyree, your Uncle Tobias fetched the bag of candy all the way out here. Now, why don't you give him a hug, then get a piece for you and Leroy and go on outside. 'Spect your uncle and Mr. Ray want to have some grown man talk."

Tyree glanced up at me and I patted him on the shoulder. “Run along now. Your uncle and I will be out in a few minutes. We need to have some old men business talk. Bore a smart boy like you.” I winked at him. He grinned and crossed the room where he hugged his uncle. Then he dug a couple of pieces of candy out of the bag and grabbed his brother by the hand.

Tobias watched the boys head out into the yard. He turned toward Vivian and smiled. It looked like a natural smile. A family smile.

“They’re both nice boys, sister. You’ve done a fine job of raising them.”

“They ain’t raised yet.”

“No,” he said, “but Tyree, he’s sure getting to be a big fellow.” Tobias shook his head. “Why, I remember when he was born. Weren’t hardly as big as a loaf of bread. Now look at him. Yes, Viv, you’ve done a mighty fine job.”

She swatted at him playfully. “Aw, you do go on, Tobias. Always did love to talk. My goodness, listen to me, blabbering on like some carnival barker. Here you done walked all the way from town and I ain’t even offered you a cool drink. I’ve got some sun tea made. You want a glass? Know your throat has to be dry.”

Tobias nodded. “Dry as dead bones. Yes, sister, a glass of sun tea would be fine.”

She smiled, stood up and smoothed her dress, then turned to at me. “How ‘bout you, Ray, you want some tea? You’ve been working in the garden all morning and you must be thirsty.”

“Tea would be nice,” I said, although I’d worked no more than an hour and wasn’t particularly thirsty. She was trying to make me look good in front of her brother, which somehow made me feel good.

She poured us each a jelly-jar full of tea. "I'll leave you gentlemen alone."

"This won't take long, Viv."

"Take your time. I'll be outside with the boys."

We watched her go. For a big woman she moved with a certain style. Grace, you could argue.

"That's one good woman," Tobias said without looking at me, "even if she is my sister."

"She's been nice to me."

He turned and fixed his eyes on mine. His eyes reminded me of smooth black stones. "Then you be nice to her."

"I wouldn't hurt her on purpose." I couldn't believe this conversation, not about a colored woman. But, then again, Vivian wasn't your average woman, at least not to me. Not anymore. Funny, I thought, how change slipped in on a man's blind side—took him unawares. Before he really caught on, well, it was too late. I wasn't exactly sure what to make of such. One thing was clear, I wasn't half as smart as I'd thought I was.

Tobias' mouth moved, but he didn't speak. Instead, he sipped at his tea. "I was planning to come out here soon, anyway. Then something happened, and I lucked into a ride with Arthur Upton. He was taking a wagon load of lumber to Jensen and I'd done him a favor a while back." He took another sip of tea, eyeing me over the rim of the jar. "Try to get out at least once a month to check on Viv and the boys. You know about the last man she had?"

"She told me."

"He hurt her bad. I won't stand for that again."

I sipped tea and stared out at the sunlight dappling the yard. The tea wasn't cold, but it was refreshing. Whiskey would have been better, but there are times a man simply has to take what's offered.

We sat quietly for a moment, listening to the birds in the oaks and the murmur of happy voices out in the yard, punctuated at intervals with laughter, and maybe a little to whatever voice was talking inside our heads. The air in the room was warm and I swiped at the sweat on my face and waited for him to speak.

"Like I said, I was coming out soon anyway, but I came a few days early."

He paused and stared at me. I stared steady back at him. His face was set hard, and in the dimly lit room it was examining a hickory carving. I couldn't read him.

"Heard from a fellow I know that a couple of folks been asking about a man who sounds a lot like you."

It felt like a hammer had hit me square in the chest. "Your friend catch any names?"

"Don't believe they gave none." Tobias took another drink of tea. I watched the rise and fall of his chest. I could see where this conversation was going and thought about what I would say, and what I would do. I been waiting a long time for such news, but I won't claim I was totally ready. Thinking about doing something hard is one thing; actually doing it can be another matter entirely.

Tobias made a face. "But from his description, the woman surely must favor that photograph you showed me." He rubbed the back of his neck as if he'd been carrying a burden, a heavy one, and it had finally been lifted. Probably my imagination, but it felt like a new weight was settling on my shoulders.

"What were they asking?"

"Wanting to know if anybody had seen you."

"What reason did they give for asking?"

"According to Spense, they was trying to hook up with a long-lost friend."

I nodded. "This Spense, he reliable?"

Tobias nodded. "In the forty years I've known him, I've never caught him in no lie."

"You sure these people didn't give any names?"

"If they did, Spense didn't catch them."

"Say where they were staying?"

"Nope. Least Spense never heard it, if they did. All he heard was them asking about a man who sure sounds like you."

I thought about things for a minute. A squirrel ran across the yard and I watched him claw up the first tree. "Where did your friend hear these people asking about me?"

"Spense, he cleans up at the Jackson Bar after it closes. That night he'd got there about five minutes early and this couple, blonde woman and a man, was coming out of the bar. Blonde woman stepped out into the light on the porch, so he got a good look at her. Claimed she matched your photo mighty close. I described it to him real good, you see."

"What about the man?"

"The man, he stayed mostly in the shadow, so Spense never eyeballed him good."

A sheen of sweat had formed above my upper lip and I wiped it off. A fly was buzzing the room. His buzzing was loud. I hate flies, always crawling all over dead animals and manure.

"What night did your friend see these people?"

"Believe it was a Saturday night."

I nodded and thought about that. I didn't say anymore and neither did Tobias. He gave me a questioning look, but didn't say anything. I pulled my last pack of cigarettes out of my pocket and tapped two out. I handed one to him. He took it, nodded his thanks, and stuck it between his lips. I slipped mine between my lips. Then I struck a match and lit us both up. For a few minutes we sat smoking, and sipping, and thinking. Least I was.

When he finished his cigarette, he stood up. “Well, I’ve said what I came to say. Guess I’ll go visit with my sister for a bit.”

I nodded, and he turned and started walking.

“Tobias,” I called after him.

He turned and I pushed up and walked across the earthen floor. “Thanks for coming all this way to tell me,” I said, sticking out my right hand. He studied it for a moment, as though it was a new kind of crawdaddy, but then he took it in his and we shook hands.

“You be careful,” he said. “Spense, he said that what he could see of the man looked mean. Plus, while he couldn’t swear to it in no law court, he said it sure looked to him like he could see the butt of a pistol sticking out of the waist of the man’s britches.”

“Don’t worry,” I said. “I’ll keep both eyes open wide.”

“Do that,” Tobias said. “Do that, and don’t hurt my sister’s feelings. I’d hate to have to beat the pure living hell out of you.” He winked, grinned, and whirled on his good heel like a ballroom dancer. I watched him limp out into the sunlight. I didn’t follow. Instead, I went and lay on my back on the bed and smoked another cigarette while I thought about what I needed to do next. Making the right move was mighty important. Maybe as important as living or dying.

Thirty-six

LONG BEFORE DARK I was in place. The spot I'd picked was a shallow stand of pines that followed the curve of the hill south of the Jackson Bar. Actually, the name of the joint was the General Stonewall Jackson Bar, but most folks around town simply called it the Jackson Bar. I figured Stonewall was a hard name to say after three or four shots.

From where I sat, I had a clear view of the parking lot. Even better, I was already in deep shadow. By the time darkness fell I would be damn near invisible.

Cars were already pulling onto the gravel parking lot and headlights flickered on and off where the road curled through the second-growth pine and poplar that covered the flat land west of town. Settling back against a larger than average pine, I twisted the cap off the bottle of Moorman's. As whiskey goes it was cheap.

I wondered if they'd come. This was the second Saturday in a row I'd made that long walk. I was getting stronger every day, but my legs still tired too quickly to suit me and I stretched them out and closed my eyes. In the middle of the pines the air was dead still and I could hear mosquitoes whining. The heat of the day had gone but sweat still beaded my face and my shirt stuck to my back. I took another sip, holding the whiskey in my mouth, savoring it before I swallowed, feeling the burn all the way down my throat.

Lights flickered out of the dusk as another car pulled off the highway and crunched across the gravel. Close behind was a pickup truck with the top cut off. A man and a woman got out of the car, but she was too tall for Gladys and Johnny had never been that heavy. Three men stepped out of the pickup. All were tall and thin and wore overalls. I settled back against the tree.

Earlier in the day there had been a breeze, but about an hour ago it had died off completely. Due to some strange combination of rocks and trees and earth, the parking lot was virtually an amphitheater. Every word came to me as clear as if the speaker and I were in church.

The man and woman kissed but didn't speak. Daylight was going fast and the porch lights hadn't come on, so I couldn't see the woman's face clearly. I closed my eyes and remembered when Gladys and I used to kiss like that.

One of the three men was telling a joke. I'd been thinking about Gladys and missed some of it, but the punch line was something about what a priest, a rabbi, and a bowlegged Baptist preacher all have in common. As they meandered into the bar, the three men laughed like hyenas.

A strand of lights tacked up around the porch ceiling popped on. The lights were different colors: blue and red and yellow. I like the blue ones best. For some reason, they make me think of Christmas, and I tried to remember the last time I'd celebrated Christmas. Two more cars rolled into the lot, but only one man got out of each.

After the second man went inside, a train whistle blew and I figured it was the Saturday Special to New Orleans. I was half tempted to take off running across country and try to catch it. But I didn't know the ground and, anyway, I had unfinished business.

By the time I'd knocked off about half the bottle, night had come and the cars were pouring in. Must have been a payday at some plant. Hadn't figured there were this many people close to Broughton. Darkness covered the outer edges of the parking lot, but all I had to do was watch the door. The minute anybody stepped up on the porch, I could see their face clear enough.

Time has a knack of slipping away, especially if you're really tired and close your eyes for a minute. Only that minute stretched out like hot rubber and my mind started to go all fuzzy. A sharp sound jerked me out of a shallow sleep and I leaned forward and stared at the parking lot. A long car was pulling in and I wondered how much I'd missed.

Watching that long car, I almost missed them. Never did figure out why I glanced at the porch precisely at that moment. Movement must have caught my eye, or maybe it was an instinctive look – the way an animal will glance in a particular direction without any reason. In the final count, don't guess why mattered much. Anyway, I glanced at the porch in time to see a couple step inside. The woman's hair was the same shade of yellow certain roses are and there was something familiar about the set of the man's head on his neck. I scrambled to my feet and started picking my way down the hill.

Before I got to the bottom, the couple was inside, but I'd got enough of a look to set my blood to singing. Scent of pines was thick and sweet in the gathering dark, but all I wanted to smell was hot blood. I could almost taste its thick stickiness on my tongue.

By the time I made the parking lot there wasn't enough light left to tell one hand from the other. Headlights probed the darkness as more cars pulled in off the highway. I hadn't had the faintest that so many folks came to a roadhouse outside of Broughton, Louisiana on Saturday night. That made me wonder what else I might not know.

For the better part of an hour, I wandered around the parking lot trying to find the old car. If it was there, I couldn't find it. After studying on that for a while, it came to me that maybe Johnny had got them a new one. That idea grew on me and I got to calculating how to find out which one was theirs. I sat down on the running board of a pickup and studied on that question for a spell. When the solution came to me, I could feel my lips spreading wide in the biggest grin I'd worn in months.

Once I had my plan worked out in my brain, I let my mind drift. Never in my life have I been able to explain why my mind worked the way it did. First thing I thought about was my grandparents' old farmhouse off Highway H back in Platte County. It set back off the road about a quarter mile and a gravel road led from the road to the side yard. I remember how that gravel seemed so white to me as a kid. Always thought it was mighty pretty in the moonlight.

Then I thought about the hen house, and the old barn over the hill and the big garden beside the white house. But what I thought about most was the way my cousin and I used to climb the stairs to the second floor, where the three bedrooms were, then sit down and slide down the steps on our rear ends. Kids are mostly crazy till they grow up and get a little common sense. Joe and I used to bump down those steps, then climb right back up and do it again. We'd do that for hours, or until some grownup made us quit. Hadn't seen Joe since he took off for Washington state to pick apples in the fall of '30. I'd driven him down to the station in the buggy. It had been raining, not hard, just steady as if it aimed to go on raining for a long time. I'd stood under the eaves of the station, watching the rain drip off the roof and waving to him as the locomotive started chugging away. No way to know if he'd made it to Washington or not. We never got a letter. Not even a postcard. But then, Joe simply wasn't much of a hand to write.

As the evening wore on, my stomach started growling and I wished I had another ham sandwich like I'd eaten at lunch. An apple sounded good, too. But all I had was the whiskey and half a pack of cigarettes. Since my head was already a little fluttery, I pulled out the cigarettes and tapped one out.

By the time I had the second one lit, people were starting to drift out of the bar. A few stood around smoking or drinking, or simply shooting the breeze. It was a nice night for doing most anything. Plenty warm, with a touch of breeze now and then and a sky full of white moving clouds and a milky moon. The humidity seemed down and the scent of honeysuckle was sweet.

Thirty-seven

I HAD BEEN DREAMING ABOUT Vivian lying in her bed, a smile on her face, thinking about something, or someone special, when the closing of a car door slammed me back to wakefulness. I blinked and watched headlights popping on. Sitting up straighter, I watched a hatchet-faced man in a straw hat roll by. A minute later one man called out "Good-night. Another voice answered, "Night."

Neither voice was Johnny's, but I got my butt off the running board and worked my way around to the south side of the roadhouse to a slight rise of ground, providing myself with a good view of the entire parking lot. No trees grew on the rise, but the grass hadn't been cut in a long time, which gave me some cover, especially when I worked into the prone position. Plus, the spot was back far enough from the roadhouse that I was nothing more than one shadow among many. I eased down on my stomach and watched people come stumbling out, heading for their car or truck. I wasn't much worried. Gladys' blonde head would be almost as good as a kerosene lantern.

People were coming out steady and I was busy keeping up. A few of them were women, but all the women had dark hair, and anyway none of them favored Gladys. Gradually, the parking lot started to empty. The music inside the roadhouse died off. I got up on one knee and had a good look. Only two cars and a pickup remained in the lot and I began to be afraid they'd slipped by me. The pickup belonged to the three men in overalls who'd come before dark. If they'd been drinking all this time, I didn't see how they could drive. Maybe they planned to sleep in the truck.

A tall, burly man came out and zigzagged his way to one of the cars. He sat inside for a couple of minutes before he finally turned the key and the tires started crunching gravel. Before he was halfway down the side road, I was headed toward the remaining car. I wasn't certain, but the gamble made sense. It was a big touring car with the top down. I eased the back door open and lay down on the floorboard.

Between the seats, it was dark and quiet, and I reckon the walk had tired me out more than I'd realized, 'cause the next thing I knew I was jerked out of my dozing by the voices of men and a woman's laughter. One of the voices sounded like Johnny's. I'd have bet my life the laugh belonged to Gladys. All of a sudden, my plans seemed as full of holes as my mother's old colander, and I scrunched down lower and eased my gun out of my pocket, wondering who the other man was.

Somebody stumbled in the gravel and Gladys started laughing again. She kept on laughing until I knew she was drunk. Her laughter rubbed on my nerves like a dry corn cob moving across sensitive skin. I almost laughed myself when I remembered that I'd used to think her laugh was cute.

"Damn, John, I do believe I might have drunk a tad too much." It was the new man; I didn't know his voice.

Sounded like old Johnny had come up in the world. Now he was John, as in Lord John or Sir John. Yeah, I thought, and I knew him when.

"Might of had one too many, myself," Johnny said. Then I heard gravel crunching and the door on the passenger side screeched open. If either the third man or Gladys wanted to sit in the back, all I could hope for was that they were blind drunk. My luck never had run that good.

"I'll get in the back," the man said.

"No, you can sit up front with us. Let Gladys slide in first and then you can ride on the other side of her."

"Sure, Ted, you can sit beside me. You aren't scared of little old me, now are you?"

The driver's door swung open and somebody plopped down behind the wheel. The springs squeaked and the car rocked a little. "Hush your blabbing, Gladys, and get inside." I didn't have to see him to know that voice. I'd know it when we both hit Hell.

"What's your hurry, honey? The night's young."

"Well, I'm not. Now get in."

"All right, you old sourpuss."

The car rocked again and then I caught a whiff of her perfume and then the car rocked again. Doors slammed and the engine cranked. It didn't catch the first time and Johnny mumbled "Damn." Then he cranked it again.

It caught, Gladys shouted "Whee," and the car jerked forward as gravel crunched beneath the tires. Lying in the floor, the sound was close and loud. I could hear the tires spinning in the loose gravel and the car rocked like a drunken sailor when they hit a rut or chughole.

After a few seconds, the road smoothed and Johnny opened the engine up and I figured we were on the highway.

Not that being on the highway changed much. The third man was something I hadn't counted on. With him along my plan was shot to hell and back. My mind seemed frozen. Maybe fear had control, but I couldn't get my brain in gear.

"Johnny, baby, I looked for Ray all night, but didn't see him. Did you?"

"No, Gladys, I didn't see him."

"Who's Ray?" the third man said.

"He's the man we..."

"Hush up, Gladys. I swear, sometimes I think you could talk the names off tombstones."

The car swerved, then straightened out. "Damn possum, laying out in the middle of the road at night. They've got to be about the dumbest animal. Not to mention the ugliest," Johnny said. "That one was luck. Much as I've had to drink, it's a wonder I could miss him."

"Now, what about this Ray?"

"Oh, hell, Ted, Ray's the one I was telling you about. The guy who was trying to kill me after that last job. He's a mean son-of-a-bitch, too. Not to mention a liar. Always telling something on us, even if he has to make it up."

"Did you see him tonight, honey?"

"No," Johnny said, "but I did talk to a man who said old Ray had been in Broughton asking questions about us. We've got to be careful, I tell you. Keep an eye out."

Sure, I thought, that's about like a hyena worrying about a wounded zebra. The air seemed a touch cooler and I raised my head a couple of inches and let more wind blow across my face. That air carried scents with it, pine and cedar, dirt and dust, motor oil and hot asphalt, and sweat, whiskey, and stale perfume. Maybe I could smell a little fear, too. Or maybe that was only my imagination.

In my mind, I could see everything clearly now; all my plans were nothing more than dry, dead leaves whirling before bitter November winds. What I'd planned to do, if you could call a few stray, vague thoughts a plan, was to slip into the back of their car then rise up a couple of miles down the road in the middle of nowhere and scare the hell out of them. Then, I'd been going to shoot them. Only if they begged real pretty, I might shoot them dead with the first shot instead of letting them bleed to death slowly in a field full of brambles and horse weeds.

But I hadn't counted on the other man – the joker in the deck. For all I knew, he could have been Cain or Abel. But he'd never done me a wrong turn, so I didn't owe him a bullet. Not like I owed Johnny and Gladys. Owed them fair and square for lying to me, for carrying on behind my back, for letting me take the big risk, then trying to shoot me down like a mad dog when they made the big score. Yeah, I owed that pair a lot. And I aimed to pay. Only how?

One of the men said something I missed. Whatever he'd said, it must have been funny, because Gladys laughed again. The road began to twist like a curled-up garden hose and after a couple of minutes I couldn't even have sworn we were in Louisiana. Seemed now like my best chance was to jump out when Johnny slowed for a curve and hope the brush was close, and that alcohol had slowed their reactions. I'd been hoping to at least get a sight on where they were holed up, but now I was pure lost.

The other man began to whistle. I'd heard the tune before, only I couldn't put a name to it. Gladys spoke over the sound.

"You said something while ago about Ray looking for us in town. Was you joshing, Johnny?"

"Nope. Wish I was. Talked to a fellow tonight though that described him to a T, even down to the way he fixes his eyes on you. Like a camera, you know. As though he was taking your picture. Said old Ray asked a lot of questions about us. 'Course, that man didn't know much and I guess Ray didn't say exactly what he was looking for. Still, he described us pretty good, even down to my scar."

"What'd you say about that?" Gladys was trying to remain calm, but fear ran through her words like electrical current.

"Oh, not much. Only that he was a liar about most things, and a crook better than half the time."

The stranger laughed, but Gladys didn't. Fresh air, or fear, must have been sobering her up, because all of a sudden she was right worried about me.

"Did he say where Ray was at?"

"No, I asked. The man didn't know. But if Ray talked to one man, odds are good he talked to another. I'll go into town tomorrow and start sniffing around. Told you he didn't go far. Not with a gunshot wound. Besides, Ray wouldn't fit in most places. He takes a strange turn at times. Somebody will remember him, especially when I let them know there's five dollars for the man with good information."

The road bent and I sensed we were going north. But that was only a sensation and, short of sitting up and staring at the road and then the sky, I had no way of being sure.

"That the man you were telling me about?" the other man said.

"The very same."

"Say he aims to kill you?"

"Already tried and, sure, he'll try again. Only this time I'll be ready. If all goes right, I plan to beat him to the punch. You with me?"

"Sure," the other man said, "count me in. If there's one thing I can't stand, it's a double-crosser."

Gladys giggled and the car slowed, rumbling across metal. Easing my head another two inches higher, I could see a gap in the trees, and a church white among them and I knew where we were.

Less than two minutes later, Johnny turned the wheel left, braked to a stop and cut the motor. For several minutes, they sat in the car, jabbering and laughing. Johnny told his favorite lame joke about the old preacher who said his family was so poor when he was a boy that they had popcorn for breakfast, drank water for lunch, and swole up for supper. Everybody laughed and then somebody fired up a cigar. Seconds later, they got out of the car, trailing smoke, laughing and jabbering on their way to the house.

I counted to two hundred, backwards. Then I eased up and cautiously looked around. The moon was peeking through a crack in the clouds and I could see a cabin made of rough lumber set back off the road. Two oak trees fronted the cabin and a creek ran alongside, then bent west and disappeared around a curl of land. I could hear the murmuring of the water and see moonlight sparkling on the surface. One tall pine stood at the corner of the house, and there was a shed beyond the pine. For some time, I studied the place. After a bit, I had it fixed in my mind. When I saw it again, I would know it. I would know it all right, and then, if things worked out the way I was planning, Johnny and Gladys would know I knew it.

Smiling, I slipped out of the car and began to walk back through the night to the railroad tracks we'd crossed. Wind gusts were picking up and there was heat lightning off to the west, out toward Texas. As I hit the road, an image of Vivian flickered across my mind and I wondered if she was dreaming of me.

Thirty-eight

"I FOUND THEM."

"Here? The two you was looking for? The blonde and the fella with the scar on his chin?"

"Yeah," I said, "those two. They're out of town aways, maybe a half-mile beyond where the railroad track runs close by a church."

Tobias scratched his jaw. "West of here?'

"Yes."

"Then I reckon I know the place. 'Bout three miles out the old Culpepper Road. Years ago there was a community there. Name of Green Briar. About all gone last time I was by there, and that was two, maybe three years ago. Only buildings still standing were the church you mentioned and a couple of houses. If you know where to look, you can still see the old road where it cut in behind that church. All growed over now, but you can still see the depression."

"Is that where the, uh, Negroes lived?"

"No, it was generally white folks what lived there. Most of them was poor. Dirt farmers, that's all they was. A few of 'em owned their land, but most was sharecroppers. Used to raise some cane, and one or two had a melon patch. If I remember right, a couple tried cattle, but I don't think they had no luck. Seems like some folks purely don't have no good luck at all."

"Was downright deserted out there the other night. What happened to all the people?"

"Some got old and died and the young ones didn't want that kind of life no more, 'specially not them what had been in the war. Guess life just naturally happened. Happened like it does to all of us."

"Spect so," I said and leaned back in my chair. I took a drag off my cigarette and thought about what I wanted to say. We were sitting on the back porch of Tobias' house. Vivian and Tobias's wife were in the kitchen, chatting as they washed dishes. The kids were playing in the back yard. Some sort of a running game I hadn't figured out. "They're looking for me, too."

Tobias shifted in his chair and the chair squeaked. "How do you know?"

"Heard them talking. Johnny told the other man they were still trying to find me."

"Who's this other man?"

"Don't know. Somebody they met here, I reckon. He's staying with them, too. Least he was."

"Could be more than one new friend out there. What you gonna do about that?"

One of the boys yelled and a girl screamed. A chorus of giggles followed. Kids, I thought, crazy kids. I took another drag. "I don't know, man. That is the question."

Tobias's wife started laughing in the kitchen. She had a strong, honest-sounding laugh. One that reminded me of Gladys' laugh. I felt the anger start to rise.

"I'll have to figure out some way to get the two of them alone."

Tobias didn't say anything. The air had turned dark and I couldn't read his face. All the kids were trooping in from the yard and a whippoorwill had started up beyond the pony shed. I could hear the women again. They were singing now, some spiritual. I'd heard the song before but didn't know the name.

A memory floated on the refrain of that song. A memory of my father singing. The way I remember his singing, it was always summer and we were all sitting around on the front porch. Some in chairs or jammed up tight together on the swing, sweating and picking at one another, scratching at chigger bites. Rest of us would be sitting on the edge of the porch, our little legs dangling over the edge. In my memory, it is always evening and the stars are starting to come out. The trunk of the sycamore in the side yard is white as parchment paper against the thickening darkness. Fireflies are flickering out in the yard. Seems like my mother is there, too, and maybe some cousins, but it is always evening and a cool breeze is always blowing across the hot, tired land and my father is singing, low and humble, his voice filling my mind and my heart until my eyes burn and I have to turn away and look across the fields, all the way down to the old barn, rising like an ancient castle out of the deep blue dusk.

In my memory, my father only knows three songs, and he sings them over and over until the very last light in the world has left the sky and the stars burn cool and the moon swings low and the fireflies flicker on and off like lightning dots. My father always keeps singing. Singing "The Battle Hymn of the Republic," "Church in the Wildwood," and "Way Down in Missouri." Singing them in the sweet evening breeze, singing them to himself, to his family, to all the birds and cattle and the lonely white stars above. Singing them as hymns of praise. Singing them as an expression of purest joy. Singing them against the coming of the night.

"You're doing a powerful lot of thinking over there."

Tobias' voice startled me and I felt the flesh on my arms pucker and the blood flash hot and angry inside my body. I took a deep breath and coughed a little, purely to clear my throat, see. Well, maybe to also give me a few seconds to journey all the way from Missouri to Louisiana.

"Trying to figure how to get things arranged." I'd been giving a good deal of thought to how to pull everything off and was beginning to wonder if I wanted to meet them on their home ground.

"That's always the hard part, at least I've found it that way. Doing sort of comes natural once you have everything set up."

"Yeah," I said, "the doing's going to come natural, sweet and natural."

As the kids trooped up the steps, the big man spoke to each, or rubbed their nappy heads, or swatted their little tails. They were all laughing and giggling, asking for licorice or a soda pop or a penny, rolling their eyes the whole time and making monkey faces. After they'd passed, Tobias put his hands on his knees and leaned toward me. I could smell his sweat and tobacco, but all I could see of his face were the whites of his eyes and his teeth when his lips moved.

"You aiming to do it all yourself?"

That was a good question. One I'd been studying on all evening. "Reckon so," I said, "provided I could get someone to start things off a little."

"What you mean, start things off?"

"Way I see it, if next time those two were in town asking about me and someone was to tell them that they'd heard of a man sounded a lot like me living at a certain place, that might get things started."

"You mean send them off on a false trail, only you'll be waiting at the end of that trail?"

"That's about the size of it," I said. Taking a long drag off my cigarette, I sucked smoke halfway down my lungs, then blew it back out.

"Be like a surprise for them, see. They come around some bend in the road and there would be old Ray, smiling like he had good sense and was powerful pleased to see them."

I whistled a little bit of "When Johnny Comes Marching Home" before I turned and peered across the darkness at Tobias, or rather the little I could see of him. "I sure do like surprises, don't you?"

He laughed and said, "I surely do, and, what's more, I think I know exactly the spot you're looking for."

I nodded, grinned, and started whistling that old marching tune again. Tobias joined in and we whistled as the breeze cooled our hot faces. Whistled to the owls, and the frogs, and the cat stretched out on the front porch, whistled in praise and pure joy, whistled against the coming of the night. And I thought again of my father. And I wanted to cry.

Thirty-nine

"DON'T DO THIS, RAY?"

"I have to, Viv."

"No, you don't. Killing ain't right. Killin's a sin. Says those very words right in the Holy Bible. Old Testament and New. Thou shalt not kill, why, that's one of the Ten Commandments."

We were standing beneath one of the live oaks. Daylight had almost gone and the night birds had started singing. I walked to the edge of the line of trees and looked across the cleared ground to the house. Both boys were inside. Worry had laid on my shoulders like a wool blanket since I'd heard Johnny and Gladys were so close, hunting for me.

Without taking my eyes off the house, I said, "Commandments are for those who believe in them, and we already know that those two don't keep very many of the ten. Already, they've stolen and lusted and committed adultery. Not to mention, they would've killed me if they could have. No, baby, I sure don't plan on trusting them to honor the Ten Commandments. Only trust them as far as I would a rattlesnake under the covers with me at night."

"But Jesus..."

"But Jesus nothing. Look around, Viv. Do you see Jesus here? Is God going to reach out and smite Johnny and Gladys dead? Huh? What do you think? Well, I don't think so. Had an old uncle back in Missouri who always was saying that the Lord helps those who help themselves, and it sure seems to me like he was right."

I turned and looked at her, a darker shadow within shadows. Only her eyes were visible; they glittered like wet stones.

"Face it, honey, if I don't get them, they're going to come after me and then who knows, maybe you, maybe even the boys. Once they start asking questions and getting answers, it won't take Johnny long to put the puzzle together. Grant you, he's a lot of things, but stupid ain't one of them." I stepped deeper into the shadows, reaching for her and she came into my arms, warm and soft and shivering. I hugged her tight. Her face pressed against mine.

"But I'm afraid, Ray. I don't want to lose you."

"You won't lose me," I said, wondering as I did if I was speaking a lie. If anybody had told me six months ago that I'd be standing outside in the middle of a Louisiana night hugging and kissing on a colored woman, I'd have beat the mortal hell out of their lying ass, and made them like it. Even now, I couldn't quite believe I was doing it. It was as if I'd gone crazy, or fever had warped my brain. Or maybe there was something to all that voodoo talk. On the other hand, maybe certain things were simply beyond explaining and this was one of them. I loved her. Simply couldn't help but do that. Color didn't matter, black or white skin, it made no difference. What mattered was the person inside the skin. They could be good or bad or somewhere in between, regardless of their race. Slow as I was, I'd learned that much. Also had learned that no man knows all truths. I pressed my lips against her forehead. “No baby, you ain’t gonna lose me. I aim to make damn sure that doesn’t happen, whatever it takes.”

“But you don’t know. You said they was pure mean. Things can go wrong, you know.”

“I agree. That’s why I ain’t gonna take no chances. I’m gonna be there waiting for them when they come sneaking up before daylight to send me to my maker. There’ll be a surprise all right, only the surprise is going to be on them. Tobias has laid it on thick, and I know Gladys. She’ll jump at the bait like a chicken jumping on a Junebug. Now, old Johnny, he might be more cautious on his own, but he ain’t on his own, is he? No, baby, this is going to work. It’s the only plan that’ll work. Leastways the only plan I could think of. You got anything better?”

Her head moved back and forth across my chest. “No, but I still don’t like it.”

“I don’t either,” I said, “but we’ve got to do something. Surely, you can see that.”

Vivian didn’t say anything. Only hugged me tighter as we swayed in shadows so thick they felt like down comforters. I could smell the bayou: rotting plants and decomposing fish, plus a dozen more odors I couldn’t name. A puff of breeze blew up and rattled the leaves on the live oaks. Lifting Vivian’s face, I kissed her soft lips. They tasted warm and sweet. Off in the timber, an owl hooted. That surely was one lonesome sound.

Forty

I CAME OUT of the dream kicking and gasping, still half lost, not knowing where I was. Fear sweat covered my face. The only light was pale and weak and I was lying on damp ground, surrounded by a thicket of green saplings. A fine mist swirled beyond the saplings and, peering through the mist down a sloping meadow, I could see an old sharecropper shack with a dirt road running in front of it. A shaft of wind blew the mist apart and I could see cane fields beyond the shack. In first daylight, the cane was dully purple. When I saw that cane, I knew where I was.

It was daylight and they were coming. Johnny and Gladys were coming. They expected me to be asleep in that old shack next to the cane field. Tobias had spread the word so thoroughly that three or four men must have given them the same answer, and now they were coming.

All I had to was watch the road and when I saw their car, work my down the slope. A depression cut across the length of the slope. It wasn't a ditch; it was more as though, back in the time before man, the earth had shifted, one patch of ground separating from the other by a couple of feet.

Since then, grass had covered both patches of ground. Grass and Queen Anne's Lace and cornflowers. Cornflowers had always been my mother's favorite.

Something told me to start moving. Maybe my ears had caught a sound so faint it didn't consciously register. Or call it instinct. Gut feel was the one thing I always trusted. I pushed off the ground and started moving.

Forty-one

I WAS BENT OVER LIKE an old man, but moving quickly, somewhere between a fast walk and a lope. The downhill slant made the going easy. All I had to do was watch my footing and not stumble. Over the sound of my breathing, I could hear the car clearly. It sounded like an old rattletrap and I remembered when Johnny and I first started in together we'd always talked about driving only Cadillacs when we hit the big time. Turned out the big time was nothing but a big joke. Except nobody was laughing.

At the bottom of the slope was the natural ditchline and I turned and hurried along it for maybe fifteen yards, then hustled up the slope and crossed the road in a dead run. Off to the near side of the house was a forsythia bush that hadn't been trimmed in years. It had grown monstrous and was flanked on both sides by massive gum trees. This part of the yard was slightly uphill from the house and from behind the forsythia I could see the driveway and the front yard without any problem. I'd checked that out the day before. As I crossed the side yard, I drug the pistol out of my belt.

The road to the old place rose and fell as if it had been built on an ocean. The car motored down into one of the dips. I could hear it and see a thin curtain of dust, but the car itself was out of sight. I eased in behind the forsythia, got down on one knee, and parted the branches. The gravel drive was half-choked with weeds, but I could see it clear. A west wind was rising like it was blowing in trouble and a shutter banged against the side of the house.

An old rope swing dangled from a maple around back and what was left of a hen house leaned heavily toward New Orleans. You could make out where the garden had been and there were gooseberry bushes growing along the edge of it. The outhouse still stood and the path leading to it wasn't overgrown so bad that you couldn't make it out. An old-fashioned white rose had climbed all over a wooden trellis. What with all the trees and bushes and the roses still blooming and the way it sat sweet between the white dusty road and the purple cane fields, you could see that it had once been a pretty place. Now, with the sagging fences and the paint peeling off and the weeds choking the garden, it had a forgotten, woebegone air. Struck me as a sad thing to let a nice place go like that. For a moment, I wondered about the people who had lived there over the years, and whether they had been happy, or sad. Then the car topped the last rise and I didn't have time to think about the old place anymore.

The sun had crested the top of the knoll and a single beam of light shot down the road like a Hollywood searchlight. Only all it hit was the windshield of the rattletrap Ford. The glare was blinding.

The pistol was suddenly heavy and I could feel sweat worming its way down my back in spite of the early morning chill. Then the ground started shaking and my first thought was earthquake. But when I glanced down, I could see it was only my legs trembling.

When I looked back up, the car was wheeling on by the house and I felt foolish. Then it began to slow before turning in a wide space where somebody might have kept a cow or horse years ago. I eased to my left, working my way deeper into the forsythia. Sunlight, cruelly bright so soon after the night, filled my eyes, half-blinding me, and I blinked, squinted, and hunkered down, changing the angle, trying to see faces.

Both doors opened and figures emerged. That's all they were, only silhouettes, black against the rising sun. The driver stretched and rolled his head around like his neck had a crick in it. He was about Johnny's height, but bigger through the chest. I started to wonder.

"Ain't you gonna shut it off, Ted?"

The voice made me jump and forsythia leaves rustled around my shoulders. It was the passenger who had spoken, and it had been a man's voice. Nothing more than a hoarse stage whisper, but enough. Don't know why my mind had been so set on Gladys being there. There had been another man with them at the bar and when you thought about things, it made a whole lot of sense in having another man along instead of Gladys. Oh, she could handle a gun well enough. In fact, she was a pretty fair shot. I ought to know—I'd taught her. Still, she was a nervy sort and Johnny wouldn't want a partner he was worried about. That's why we'd been such a good team.

"Nah, this won't take long, and, besides, we might want to make us a fast getaway."

Funny thing—neither of those voices was Johnny's. My guts started curdling.

The men left the doors ajar and the motor running. They eased up to the house like they were coming up on a covey of quail. In the first true light of morning, I felt exposed, naked. Part of me wished it was still dark enough to slip away.

For the first twenty yards they both walked straight toward me. Then the driver made a sweeping motion with his arm and the other man broke off and headed toward the cane field at a dog trot. He was going to swing around and come at the house through the back door—easy enough to figure that out that plan. The driver was still heading directly toward me. With every step he looked less like Johnny. I brought the gun up and pointed the barrel at his chest. Before daylight I'd had nothing in the world against the man. Now, if he took three more steps toward me, I was going to have to kill him. Life gets funny that way. Well, I thought, it was his own doing. He had no call to drive all the way out here to kill me. The man had dealt the cards; now he had to play his hand. My finger tightened on the trigger.

The birds were waking up, twittering in the gum trees. The man walking toward me heard them, too, and he looked up, then began to ease around to his right. In a crouch now, keeping low, he was headed for the corner of the house. Sunlight struck the side of the house as he closed in, revealing how dilapidated it was. The evening before, right at dusk, I'd taken a tour of the place. A living room, two small bedrooms, and a kitchen with the cast iron stove still standing. Dust coated the empty floors. Mice scampered before my boots and old newspapers lay in shreds in the corners. Rain had gotten in and the floors were going rotten. Smells of mold, damp wood, and animal nests swirled together until I wondered how anybody had ever lived there. Whoever the crouching man was, he wasn't going to find what he was expecting. Grinning, I eased a few inches left, trying to keep him in view.

He was past me now and I swung the pistol with him, the hole pointed straight at his spine. He was moving slowly now, almost on tiptoe, easing up to the house. One step, another, one more, and then his hand reached up and touched the side of the old house. He lifted his head and looked around as though he sensed somebody watching. But it was only God, and me. And God didn't seem to care much what the man did and I'd suddenly figured out I needed to be somewhere else in the worst way. Silently, I urged the man to hurry.

He took his time, and I couldn't blame him. No telling what crap Johnny and Gladys had told him. For all he knew, a desperate armed man was waiting for him inside the house.

At the porch now, he eased one foot up onto the floorboards and waited for the sound of movement inside. He waited what seemed like a long time. I could feel my heart pounding against the wall of my chest. Finally, he pushed off and stepped up on the porch. As he eased his way to the door, I risked a quick glance toward the back of the house. I couldn't see the other man. I wondered if he was coming in the back door.

The man on the porch stretched out his free hand and put it on the door knob. A gun filled his other hand. His fingers found the door knob and he twisted. The door swung open. He looked around like he was expecting ghosts. Then he eased one leg inside. When his back disappeared, I started running hard for the car. A few seconds was all I could count on.

My hands were on the steering wheel when I heard the first shout. Shifting into gear, I ducked as low as I could, cranking the window down like my life depended on it. The old Ford must have been doing twenty-five or thirty when they both came busting out the front door. At the first flash of movement, I squeezed the trigger. The sound startled me, though I'd been expecting it. A gun fired right next to your head is painfully loud, especially inside an automobile.

I wasn't counting on hitting anything. If I winged the house, I'd be lucky. All I wanted to do was scare the hell out them and buy myself enough time to get out of range.

Out of the corner of my left eye, I could see them diving for the floorboards. I punched on the accelerator and eased my head even lower. I'd counted to six before I heard the first shot. My head scrunched down on my neck and I wished I was built like an old turtle and could draw my head inside my shell.

They were shooting crazy fast now and I heard one bullet ping off the Ford. They should have been shooting for the tires, and maybe they were, but I was twisting the steering wheel hard, whipping the old car back and forth, and it sure wasn't setting still.

As the sounds of gunfire grew fainter, I began to breathe easier. Then I remembered where I needed to be and my breath caught in my throat and I lifted my head and jammed the accelerator on down. Sweat popped out on my head like water bullets. As the crow flies, it wasn't that far. But I was no crow and the road was long and winding. All I could do was keep my foot pressed to the floor when I could and pray. Prayer was no sure thing. Knew that for personal certain. Wasn't sure I believed much in prayer. But there was no sense in not saying a short one. What could it hurt?

Forty-two

TIME HAS A FUNNY way of playing tricks on a man. Seemed the harder I pressed on the gas pedal the slower the car rolled and the faster time moved on. No matter how I cussed, or screamed, or beat on the steering wheel, I just couldn't seem to get where I needed to be. In a way I didn't know what was going on—not for certain, anyway. Yet, in a different way, I had never known anything more clearly in my life.

They'd set me up, or at least covered all their options. One way or another, they'd planned to take me out of the picture. Either they got me at the old sharecropper's house or they came for me at Vivian's place. How they'd found out about her place I couldn't say. But they had; knew that down in my bones. Probably Johnny had finally asked the right question.

I'd begun to think I'd never see that damn tree. Biggest catalpa tree ever, Viv had said. I knew what a catalpa tree was. They grew back in Weston and I'd seen them when Dad had driven us to town on Saturday. Only, we'd called them

Indian cigar trees. Professor down to Warrensburg had one in his yard and he'd told me the official name one time when I was doing some roofing for him.

The first road had been gravel, and I couldn't make time for fear of sliding off into the ditch or flipping over on the curves. When I'd finally hit the main road, I'd turned the nose toward the sun and floored it. But that old Ford was no speed demon. Truth was, it wasn't much of a car. Radiator was starting to steam now and if that tree didn't show up on the horizon soon, I was in a bad way. I was sweating like a race horse and I reached up and swiped the dash with the palm of my right hand. Was planning on needing that palm dry.

The radiator started hissing and, going into a sharp curve, I eased off the gas. Plowed ground lay off to the right and cattle grazed in the field to the left. As I came out of the curve, I punched the gas and the radiator blew to hell and back. But, through the steam, I could see a huge tree on the side of the road about half a mile ahead. There was a car parked a few yards beyond the tree. I eased off on the gas and coasted as far as I could. Then I maneuvered the Ford to the side of the road, swung the door open, and started running.

I'd never taken the shortcut before, but Viv and Tyree had both talked about it, so I had a good idea of where I was going. The ground sloped down toward the bayou and I could already see the tops of some live oaks. Figured they were the same ones that grew just beyond the cabin. Even if I was wrong, I wasn't far off. I swung my legs over the sagging fence and took off running again.

They'd cut hay recently and the stubble made for thick going, but I could smell the bayou now, and that, coupled with the fear, drove me on. The pistol kept banging against my leg and my breath came in gasps. I wasn't thinking about much except the need to get there yesterday. My heart was hammering like a jazz drummer beating his skins and there was a stitch down my right side. But none of that mattered. I hoped I was wrong about what was going on at the cabin, but I didn't really think I was.

For a short cut, it sure took a long time. Beyond the hayfield there was patch of corn, then a little creek, and beyond the creek a pine thicket. By now, I was tired, soaked with sweat, and scratched up from the briars and tree limbs. I was doubting myself when I broke through a patch of horseweeds on the far side of the pines and saw our cornfield, and, beyond the tasseled cornstalks, the cabin.

I stopped at the edge of the horseweeds, catching my breath and scouting out the ground. The cabin stood in a pool of sunlight and the live oak leaves shimmered green. I could hear a jay calling close by and a cow bawling back toward the road. The scene was like one of those paintings you see in a museum. Quiet and peaceful. Serene was what that Warrensburg professor would have called it.

Down along the Arkansas border, not long after the hard times hit, I'd hoboed around for a couple of weeks with an old man from Tennessee. Remember he had a long mountaineer beard and no teeth to speak of. Claimed he was kin to Andrew Jackson and was always telling stories. One I remember best ended with him saying, "Ray, the moral of that tale is believe none of what you hear and not hardly half of what you see." That was precisely the way I felt about the scene before me. I started trotting toward the cabin. I had the gun out now and was bent low at the waist like a Pawnee warrior I'd seen one time in a history book.

My breath came ragged and my heart was going crazy wild. It was so clear in my mind what was truly important to me that those visions cut like broken glass. What if I was too late? I stumbled, caught my balance, then pushed on. Sunshine covered the cabin and the yard, and made the leaves of the live oak shine like hot green money. It was also shining straight in my eyes and my face felt the way a red-hot poker glows.

Usually at least one of the boys would have been out playing in the yard or working in the garden. The place appeared abandoned. I was getting close and I slowed, cutting toward the cabin at an angle that would allow me to peep in through the kitchen window. The front door was open. I could see that now, and it spooked me. Going in through there would be about like going into a cave. A man would be half blind for at least a minute after he stepped into the dark interior, and he'd not have the faintest as to what was waiting for him.

I was up on my toes now, but my footsteps still sounded loud to my ears. Sweat ran down my forehead and stung my eyes. Swiping at it with the back of a hand, I kept moving. Going slow and low, I eased around the back, keeping crouched so that the top of my head was well below the window. Voices drifted to me now, distorted by the cabin walls.

Once I got under the window, I eased down on one knee for a couple of seconds to try and get my breath and heartbeat back under control. Then, moving slow and carefully, I eased my way up, half expecting to see the business end of a pistol pointed straight at me the second my eyes reached the window.

Inside, the cabin it was close to dark. Only the bar of light that fell through the open door broke the dimness. For a few seconds I couldn't see anything clear. Then the room began to swirl into focus.

Johnny was standing in the middle of the room, facing me. He had a gun in one hand and one finger on the trigger. Seeing his face brought back memories of when we'd been closer than blood brothers. Now we were more like Cain and Abel.

I started to duck, then noticed he wasn't looking at the window. Instead, he was staring at the far corner, in the general direction of the bed the boys slept in. From where I was, all I could see were lumpy shapes and shadows. I eased a few inches to my right and twisted my neck.

They were on the bed. Three of them. Tobias and Leroy and Tyree. Leroy was crying and shaking. Tyree was sitting with his back against the wall. His hands hung down by his sides and they were balled into fists. His face was set hard and his eyes slitted almost shut.

Tobias was on the bed, too. Only he wasn't sitting up. He was on his back and his eyes were screwed-up shut. His face looked like he'd managed to get one foot caught in the hay bailer. Only it wasn't his foot, or even his bad leg, that was hurting. The right side of his shirt was soaked with blood. He was pressing his left hand down right where his chest connected to his right shoulder. Hard to say how bad off he was, but there was no question he was suffering.

I flicked my eyes around the room. No Viv. No Gladys. I glanced again at Tobias, then back at Johnny, measuring by sight, figuring angles, calculating the odds. No matter which way I played my hand, it figured to be a loser. I couldn't trust a shot with Johnny's finger on the trigger. All it would take would be one spasm and then who the hell knew. Easing down from the window, I began to work my way around toward the front door.

Johnny was talking some and I was trying to listen to him, keep an eye out for Viv and Gladys, and stay quiet, all at the same time. Still, I could catch a bit of what Johnny was saying. Sounded as though he was asking a question. Once, for sure, I heard my name. The women were nowhere to be seen.

Don't know how long it took me. Maybe a minute. Seemed longer, but when I made the door, I was afraid to stick my head into the open space. Part of me was afraid Johnny had heard me, and part of me was afraid the boys would see me first and panic. I could hear Johnny plain now. I held my breath and listened hard.

"All right, nigger man, tell me where my old buddy Ray is."

"Done told you, I don't know." Pain threaded thick through Tobias' voice. Sounded as if he was biting down on barbed wire. Didn't have to look at him to know he was hurting bad.

"Want another bullet to go with the one I already gave you?"

"Can't tell you what I don't know."

"Don't bullshit me, boy. Know for a fact he's been to your house and you been asking about me all over town. According to you, he's supposed to be living way the hell over on the other side of that damn swamp, but something about that don't smell right. Ray being all the way over there by himself, and I know for a fact that he was gunshot not long ago. Shot up pretty bad, too. Had to have had doctoring of some kind to survive. Even if it was witch doctoring. No, nigger, something don't smell right. I figure that story for a setup. Now, for the last time, where is my old buddy?"

"Told you, I don't know."

"You're fixing to die, nigger. And for nothing. Once I get you out of the way, I'm going to start in on these boys and that won't be pretty."

"Go ahead. Shoot me. See if I care," Tyree said. His voice was quivering, but he spit the words out clear enough.

Right then I sure was proud of that boy. Proud as if he was my own flesh and blood. Tobias groaned and Leroy started sobbing and I stepped around the corner.

Don't know if something in their faces changed or if Johnny heard something that didn't sound right. Maybe he only sensed me the way a wild animal will sense danger, but Johnny whirled around and the gun was pointed straight at my gut. Well, that made us even – mine was pointed straight at the middle of his chest.

"Well, well, well, look what just showed up, and right on time, too. You couldn't have timed it any better, old buddy."

I stared at his face. It was a face I'd seen every day for more than three years. When you spend almost all your waking hours with anyone for more than a thousand days you get to know their face mighty damn well. When you are like I was and without a mirror for almost that whole time, you get more used to their face than to your own. In a way, despite the bad he'd done me, it seemed a shame to have to shoot him. But that was simply being sentimental. I can be overly sentimental if I don't watch it. At the moment, I couldn't see any choice beyond pulling the trigger.

Tobias moaned and I caught a flicker of movement. I started talking to cover it.

"Drop the gun, Johnny. Let's not make this any worse than it already is."

"No way, Ray. Tell you what, old buddy, you drop yours and you and I will take a nice walk into those trees out back."

"Where's the woman?"

"Man, you sound sweet on her. Don't tell me you've gone nigger crazy."

"Don't worry about me. Where's the woman?"

"She's with Gladys. They're going to have some nice girl talk." He grinned. For the first time, I noticed he was missing a couple of teeth. Funny what a man sees but doesn't really notice. "Maybe she'll be a little more friendly than old black Joe here."

More movement, and I stepped sideways to distract Johnny. No matter what else, he was no dummy. He blinked as I moved and his finger tightened on the trigger.

"Don't do it, Johnny."

"Ray, you know I hate to, but you don't leave me any choice. You know way too much and I can't have you blabbing to every hick sheriff south of the Mason-Dixon."

Part of a body grew visible behind Johnny. "I won't talk. You know I never have," I said.

He blinked, cocked his head to one side, and made a monkey face. "You got that right, pal. You won't be talking."

I started to say something, but I never the first word out. A body flung itself through the air and fell like a log on Johnny's arm. The arm that was holding the gun. I saw the gun fall from his hand.

Then everything went crazy. I flung myself at Johnny as he stumbled under the weight of Tyree. Tyree screamed and came cartwheeling over Johnny's shoulder and we collided. My knees buckled and hit the floor and rolled, ending up on my back with Tyree lying across my chest. Johnny scrambled for the gun and whirled toward us. I felt the gun still in my hand and squeezed the trigger. I wasn't thinking anymore. Not about dying, not about Johnny, not about Vivian, not about Tyree; I simply squeezed the trigger.

The roar was deafening.

I could only hear the echo of the gun.

When the echo died, I could hear the groaning.

"Damn," Johnny said. "Damn."

He was holding his gut with his left hand. Blood was pumping out between his fingers. He gazed at the blood on his hand. Then he lifted his head and staggered a step closer. His eyes turned glassy. Then they took on a faraway look.

Johnny stumbled backward and sat down. His back was against the wall and his eyes were open. Don't think he was seeing much. Or, maybe he was seeing a lot, like all of his life up to that moment. His lips came apart and his tongue slid out. It went back in as both eyes closed. "Ray," he murmured, "Ray."

His head fell forward onto his chest and he settled into himself, looking like a sack of feed with a hole in the bottom of the sack and the feed pouring out through the hole. Johnny's face looked young. Real young—like when we had first teamed up. But that had been in another life and I was way too old to cry.

"You okay, Mister Ray?" The boy whispered. No clue why he whispered. He was heavy on my chest.

"Yeah," I said. "Now, roll off me. You're mashing all the air out."

I sat up and faced the boy. "You okay?"

"Sure," he said. "I'm fine. But Uncle Tobias, well, that man shot him."

"Where's your mother?"

"With that other woman. The one that has a gun."

"Where'd they go?"

Tyree shook his head. "I don't know. All I know is that other woman said something about the swamp."

"Take care of your uncle," I said, pushing off the floor. "See what you can do about stopping the bleeding. Use anything in the house that—"

"But what about—"

I waved a hand at him and started running. My legs were shaky, but I drove forward. Leroy was crying and I heard Tobias moan, but I didn't stop. There was this feeling inside of me that there wasn't time, and that feeling was growing. My legs weren't strictly working proper, but I was running best I could for the bayou. The gun was heavy in my hand.

Forty-three

THE BAYOU WAS A BIG place and I didn't know where they were. I had no choice but to run and trust to luck. Surely, I was way overdue for some good fortune.

Way I had it figured, Gladys had marched Vivian off to work on her and try to get her to tell where I was in case Tobias wouldn't break. Didn't have a clue where she took her. I could only guess.

But I had to pick someplace, and in the end I figured Gladys would take her to the edge of the water. That way if she had to shoot it wouldn't be hard to ease the body into the water. Instinct and a guess. That's all I had. That, and the feeling that I was already too late.

~ * ~

Funny how your mind changes on you. Worse than the weather, or a woman. At least it seemed that way to me. My plan kept changing as I worked my way through the thick undergrowth along the bank of the bayou. I was out of the trees and into a patch of shiny, green, fat-leaved plants that put off a rotten smell. Every few feet, the vegetation gave out and I had to cross the slick mud bank. In the mud were footprints. Daniel Boone I wasn't, but broken leaves and footprints were easy enough to read. I was torn between wanting to hurry and needing to pause to listen to see if I could hear voices. Coming up too sudden on Gladys with a gun in her hand didn't seem like a good plan.

All the time I was moving I was saying silent prayers. If anybody had told me six months ago that the strongest desire in my life would be for a heavyset Black woman to live, I'd have called that person a liar straight to their face. Still, one truth doesn't change another. Having Vivian be all right was what really mattered to me, and I knew it now. Even could admit it. Well, at least to myself. When you think one way all your life, even if you've been wrong all along, changing your thinking is a challenge.

In the end it was the birds who showed me the way. I'd stopped ten yards short of where a small creek dribbled into the bayou. The shallow water was no more than two feet across. Don't know why I stopped. Could have easily stepped across and kept moving. Ground on both sides of the stream was muddy. Maybe I was subconsciously searching for a dry place to step. Or maybe I simply needed a breather. Or, if you can accept miracles, maybe somebody was answering my prayer.

What caught my ear was a sudden squawking, back in the trees and further west. I figured about thirty yards away. Then the squawking eased, followed by a sudden screeching. Seconds later, a flock of small dark birds whirled out of the trees, heading straight toward the sun.

Maybe I shouldn't have been so certain. Could have been a dozen reasons for the birds' sudden flight. But deep inside I knew. Without thinking, I jumped the creek and started running, staying low, following a narrow trail that wound between saplings and wild ferns as big as peach baskets.

Trees grew close to the trail and their branches hung over, allowing the leaves to slap me in the face. I ran on blind, cursing, praying, and gasping for breath all at the same time. A sycamore stood in the middle of the path and I curled around it to the right and as I broke through a patch of cane I could hear voices.

In front of me, the land rose a few feet and the voices sound like they were coming from the far side of the hillock. Tall grass covered the slope and I flung myself down and started crawling on my knees and elbows, holding the pistol out before me. As I neared the crest, I slowed and peeked over the top. For some reason, that put me in mind of a rabbit poking his head out of his warren.

The bayou had curled back on itself and now ran alongside a patch of ground that formed a natural bowl. They were standing in the bowl, maybe fifteen feet apart. Vivian was at the edge of the black water and her face was half turned toward me. A shaft of sunlight poured through the branches and her ebony skin glistened.

Gladys was facing her and, if I'd wanted to, I could have seen her face. Only I couldn't drag my eyes away from the gun at the end of her right arm. It wasn't a big gun. Big enough, though, and her finger was on the trigger.

"Now, for the last time, you dumb nigger bitch, tell me where he is. And don't tell me you don't know, 'cause I know a liar when I hear one. Besides, I done heard all about you and Ray. Didn't think you could keep that a secret, did you? Not something sick like that. Fever must have burnt his brain plum up for him to take up with the likes of you. Fat as a sow, and a nigger to boot." Gladys took a step toward the water. I tried to judge the distance. The odds appeared lousy. "Now, tell me where he is."

"I told you already. I don't know. Ray's been gone all night. Now that's the truth, whether you like it or not."

"Whether I like it or not. Why, you smart mouth bitch, you had your chance." The gun swung up and Gladys held it steady as a rock.

"Don't."

Her head jerked at the sound. I was halfway upright and had my gun pointed right at her head. My finger was on the trigger. I should have pulled it. But I hesitated. Once, I'd loved her. Or thought I had, and maybe when all the cards are counted that's the same thing. Or maybe it was because she was a woman and I'd never shot a woman. Who the hell knows? I sure don't. All I know is I didn't pull the trigger and I saw the skin on her face go taut and her right shoulder twitched. I heard the roar of the gun as the bullet caught me in the side, spinning me around like a child's top. I could feel my body falling and then a wave of pain washed through me as the world went black.

Then I was rolling down the slope with a thousand lights flickering in front of my eyes. When I hit bottom, I felt my mind shift out of me, then swirl back in.

Gladys was screaming and Vivian was screaming and maybe I was screaming, too. But the gun in my hand was swinging up and this time I squeezed the trigger and Gladys fired back. The whole world seemed to explode.

She turned like a French ballet dancer and I saw her glance at the sun. Then her head swung down and her eyes fixed on mine. Her lips moved, but no words came out. She fell hard into grass so green you'd swear it had been painted.

~ * ~

It took me two tries and some help from Vivian, but I made it to my feet. I bit my lip, stumbled forward four or five steps and stood there, swaying, staring down at Gladys. The front of her blouse was crimson and her lips were puckered as if she was going to kiss somebody. But the only kiss she had left was the kiss of death. Bubbles of blood swelled up between her lips and a stream of blood ran down her face. I wanted to say some meaningful words, and I think she did, too. Only neither one of us spoke. Death had robbed her of the power of speech, and, in the end, I concluded silence was, indeed, golden.

In the end, all I did was stand there, staring down at her, remembering our times together—good and bad—watching the lights dim in her eyes. When they went out, I turned and Vivian came to me. I put one arm across her shoulders and we started hobbling back toward the house. I told her the boys and Tobias were going to make it, but that was all I could get out right then.

"What am I gonna do with you, Ray? You keep getting yourself shot to pieces and all I can do is watch you suffer and bleed, then try to doctor you best as I can. Come on, baby, let's get you home."

The frogs started up then, croaking loudly deep down in the bayou. I could smell the blood and the mud, and my eyes kept flickering, and my side felt like it was on fire. I knew I had to keep moving. Moving on toward that house and people who cared about me, regardless of color.

At last, after all the lost years, I had a woman who truly loved me. And I didn't give a good hot damn if she was fat and Black. Hell, I was no movie star, either. Vivian cared about me, surely more than I deserved, and she would take care of me, and I aimed to be good to her, and true.

"Judge not, lest ye be judged." I think those words are in the Bible, and maybe they were a good, tight fit for old Missouri Ray.

Pain was coming strong now and I tried to breathe through it, saying her name to myself like a blessing. When we stepped into the shade of a sycamore that must have been young when all there was in bayou country were Indians and alligators, I quit walking. Not forever. Only long enough to bow my head and kiss her soft, quivering lips. As our lips met, I could taste her tears. They tasted like salt. They tasted like love.

Meet Chris Helvey

Chris Helvey is the author of a dozen novels and poetry collections, including the novels *Yard Man, Dancing on the Rim, Violets for Sergeant Schiller, and The White Jamaican*, all of which are available from Wings ePress. He is a founding member of the Bluegrass Writers Coalition, a contributing columnist to the Frankfort *State-Journal,* and the editor-in-chief of *Trajectory Journal.* Chris welcomes comments and suggestions from his readers. He can be reached at adobechris@hotmail.com

Other Works from the Pen of

Chris Helvey

Yard Man: A lonely man simply trying to survive The Great Depression, suddenly stumbles into a job he doesn't want, falls in love with a prostitute who doesn't love him, and incurs the wrath of the most dangerous man in Mississippi.

Dancing On The Rim: The story of one man's journey across a violent wilderness, a journey of revenge, retribution, and a search for redemption.

Violets For Sergeant Schiller: A young German Poet is swept up in the maelstrom of World War I.

The White Jamaican:_A private eye is hired to find a husband who has mysteriously disappeared.

Into the Wilderness: A middle-aged man life ruptures and he returns to his hometown in a search for peace, happiness, and a place to belong

Last Train to Miami: A Mafia hitman from Philly is sent to Miami by his Boss to do a hit for the Miami boss. Only when he arrives, he discovers that even among the Family truth can be an elusive creature.

Dear reader,

I hope you've enjoyed reading this compelling story as much as I enjoyed writing it.

Your opinion is valuable to other readers like you, who may be looking for books like mine.

Please consider taking a few minutes to post a review, however brief, on the site where you purchased this book or on the Wings ePress web page.

You may also want to visit my author page at the Wings' website, where you can find all the other books I've written.

Thank you!

Chris Helvey

Visit Our Website

For The Full Inventory
Of Quality Books:

Wings ePress, Inc

Quality trade paperbacks and downloads
in multiple formats,
in genres ranging from light romantic comedy to
general fiction and horror.
Wings has something for every reader's taste.
Visit the website, then bookmark it.
We add new titles each month!

Wings ePress, Inc.
3000 N. Rock Road
Newton, KS 67114

Made in United States
North Haven, CT
08 September 2023

41326842R00143